STEVE FEASEY

CHANGELING

ZOMBIE DAWN

MACMILLAN CHILDREN'S BOOKS

First published 2011 by Macmillan Children's Books
a division of Macmillan Publishers Limited
20 New Wharf Road, London N1 9RR
Basingstoke and Oxford
Associated companies throughout the world
www.panmacmillan.com

ISBN 978-0-330-51789-8

1 3 5 7 9 8 6 4 2

A CIP catalogue record for this book is available from
the British Library.

Typeset by Nigel Hazle
Printed and bound in the UK by CPI Mackays, Chatham ME5 8TD

For Big Al.
Thank you for your unwavering belief and support

PROLOGUE

Caliban allowed the dead body of the woman to slip from his grasp and crumple to the floor at his feet, his victim's head hitting the hard stone with a dull thud. Unseeing eyes, already bereft of the life they once reflected, stared back at him accusingly, but he paid no attention to the reproachful look as he rose from his chair and moved towards the window. Already lost in his thoughts, he slowly drew his hand over blood-smeared lips, painting a ghastly, coppery, circus-clown's grin across his face.

The vampire stared out on to the impenetrable curtain of grey mist that swirled and danced before him. Beyond that curtain lay the human realm, although technically he himself was in a part of the Netherworld which had been translocated here to Iceland by his former sorceress, Gwendolin. The Tower of Leroth had remained in this place ever since he'd abandoned it after the werewolf boy had killed Gwendolin and the tower's powers had been lost along with her. But not, as the vampire had at first thought, forever. He stared out into the slow swirling mist again, his mind forming patterns and pictures in the murk.

He was in a strange mood. Mental exhaustion from planning what lay ahead had made him edgy and introspective, and a small part of him wanted nothing more than to walk out through those grey shutters, enter the human realm and disappear: to hunt and feed undetected among his prey, as he had done for centuries, and leave behind the gruelling struggle for power that he was currently involved in. It was tempting to simply vanish but he knew that it was not his destiny. He was fated for greater things. He was to be the first lord of *two* realms: the human and the demon. And he would rule them both ruthlessly. But the struggle to achieve this aim was onerous, even for a creature like himself. He had a stranglehold on the Netherworld now. Those weak and gutless demon lords – the so-called rulers of the dark realm – had all fallen to him. Now it was the turn of the humans.

Caliban's new sorceress, Helde, had brought them here, opening a portal in the Netherworld for them to slip through. She had done so artfully, creating several decoy portals along with the one they were to use – too many for his altruistic do-gooder of a brother to check them all.

And now they were at the Tower of Leroth. Alone. Caliban had considered contacting some of his vampire brethren to join him to ensure that the tower would not be without a guard presence of some kind, but Helde had insisted that concealment was their greatest weapon, and that it should not be compromised in any way.

Helde claimed that the tower was key to their plans, that it was more than just a means of translocation and that other secrets were hidden within its walls – secrets that would help them achieve their aim of subjugating the human realm and everyone in it forever.

A sound at the door made him stiffen, and the next thing he knew the sorceress had pushed it open and stepped inside. It was unlike him to be caught unawares like this, and he inwardly cursed himself for allowing it to happen. He kept his back to her, but when he spoke the anger in his voice was obvious. 'In future, you will knock and wait at the door until I tell you to enter. Is that clear?' Caliban turned from the window to glare at the sorceress who stood looking back at him.

'Is that clear?' he repeated.

'Yes. I am sorry. I forgot.'

She was a sight to behold. Every part of her was made up of hundreds of thousands of insects, each living creature clutching on to its neighbours to form a whole – a swarming, crawling, teeming resemblance of the human female she'd once been. She had been beautiful before they had burned her human body at the stake and Caliban thought – even in this grotesque reconstituted form – her beauty was still evident. He watched as small sections of the sorceress continuously dropped off, the insects hitting the floor with a hard little *snick!* before scurrying back to rejoin the writhing, fluid mass. Her various component parts were incapable of perfect adhesion, and this flaking-off of insects was a source of great distress to Helde: the more agitated she became, the greater the cascade of invertebrates falling from her. Judging by the flow of tiny creatures tumbling to the floor at her feet now, Caliban reasoned that her latest attempt to find the thing she was looking for had been unsuccessful.

'You have failed again?' he asked, knowing that the phrasing of the question was sure to ignite her ire.

'This place!' She threw an arm up in frustration, and Caliban could not help but smile as two fingers of the hand flew off, the insects raining down on to the floor behind her before scuttling back to their comrades. 'It is a warren! These upper floors are not a problem. One staircase leads up, another down, and all the rooms have been searched thoroughly. But below, down in the lowest levels where all of those tunnels are cut through the rock . . .' She shook her head. 'There are more tunnels beneath *them*! The Shield exists. Skaleb could never have won the Demon Wars without it. The tower was too susceptible to attack otherwise. I *will* find it. It is down there somewhere.'

Skaleb had been the original owner of the tower, many centuries ago. But such history was of little concern to Caliban. The vampire sighed theatrically. 'I tire of this fruitless searching of yours. The thing you seek is little more than a distraction from our main business.'

The sorceress shook her head. 'I thought you would welcome the chance to protect yourself fully in this place. Especially after you were attacked within its confines so recently.'

The vampire shot her a look. He had no wish to be reminded of how the tower had been penetrated by the lycanthrope boy Trey Laporte, and how he had lost Gwendolin at the hands of the teenager. He had almost killed the boy that day . . . almost, but not quite. The lycanthrope was a thorn in the vampire's side. Convinced by Caliban's brother that he was the creature spoken of in an ancient legend – the key figure in thwarting the vampire in his plans to rule the human realm – the boy had an annoying habit of turning up when least expected. And so far he *had* been responsible for frustrating the vampire. He shook his head. As soon as his current plans were underway, he would make it his personal mission to remove the boy forever and put paid to the ridiculous legend.

'Nevertheless, I feel it is taking up too much time,' the vampire replied. 'Gwendolin knew nothing of this "Shield".'

'That woman? Pah! She was an amateur. Little more than a dabbler in dark magic.'

'She managed to learn many things about Leroth. It was she who rediscovered most of its secrets. Maybe you think too little of her.' He paused, eyeing the sorceress. 'Or maybe too much of yourself.'

'Do not goad me, vampire. You would do well to remember who I am and what I am capable of.'

Caliban's eyes took on a terrifying aspect, and his nostrils flared as if he could scent the blood he so adored. The vampire disappeared suddenly, reappearing directly before the sorceress. The attack was unexpected and cruel. She gasped as he plunged his hand – the real one, not his blade-fingered prosthetic appendage – into her chest, grasping her ancient heart – the heart that he had discovered and used to reanimate her. He gripped the ancient organ, squeezing it cruelly and eliciting a wail of agony from the sorceress. As his fingers squeezed, it was as if the outer glue that bound Helde together became unstuck – the trickle of insects turned into a torrent, and the sorceress seemed to melt before his eyes. Caliban leaned in, his face jammed up close to what was left of her face, and when he spoke it was in a cruel, fierce whisper.

'I am your *master*. I brought you back from the dead and I can just as easily return you there, for good. *You*,' he squeezed the heart a little harder and another terrifying screech filled the room, 'would do well to remember who *I* am and what *I* am capable of.'

He let go and stood back, watching as Helde's body slowly reformed before his eyes.

The sorceress dropped to her knees, her chest heaving as she sucked in huge breaths. Eventually she looked up at the vampire.

'You are right . . . master.' She spat out the last word. 'Forgive me. I forgot myself. It will not happen again.'

The vampire nodded. 'Good,' he said, turning away from her and walking back in the direction of his throne. He sat and imperiously raised a metal-bladed finger in the air. 'I will give you one more day to find this Shield. After that we will turn to the matter of creating our zombie army and proceed without the Shield if need be. In case you had forgotten, I plan to take over a world. Our unleashing of the undead is the first step in achieving this, and I do not want you to be distracted. Do you understand me?'

'Perfectly.'

'Then let us hope that you can live up to *both* our expectations.'

Helde opened her mouth as if to say something, but thought better of it. Instead, she slowly pulled herself up off the floor, turned on her heel, and left the room.

1

Trey Laporte left the luxurious penthouse apartment where he lived with Tom and Alexa and Lucien, took the elevator to the ground floor and stepped out past the security guards at the front door into the bright daylight. He stopped and took a deep breath, glad to be outside and away from the stuffy, air-conditioned environment inside the converted warehouse building behind him. He considered sending Alexa a text to let her know he'd gone out (he'd left without telling anyone – something his guardian, Lucien, always frowned upon) but he needed some space and time to be alone with his thoughts. The apartment, in fact the entire building that housed Charron Enterprises Inc., was nothing short of chaotic at the moment. He turned to his right and began to walk, head down, lost in thought, moving in the direction of the City.

It was already hot outside. He'd spent the early morning in the gym, sparring with a Shadow Demon friend of his, hoping that the fight training would take his mind off things. It hadn't. He'd emerged bruised and battered, showered and decided to come out for this walk.

After about twenty minutes, with Docklands well behind him, he paused and turned his face towards the sun, closing his eyes and enjoying its warmth. He ignored the pushing and jostling of the tourists who swarmed around him now that he was close to the Tower of London. It was half-term, and the usual throng of foreign visitors who flocked to this historic site were joined by parents and youngsters making the most of the sunshine in the capital city.

There was a tap on Trey's shoulder and he spun round, tense and alert. His heart hammered against his ribcage, and he eyed the oriental man in front of him, quickly scanning the area about him to see if he were a lone attacker or part of a larger group.

'*Sumimasen,*' the elderly man said, smiling and nodding in Trey's direction.

Trey was tightly wound, and the man seemed to sense this, his friendly expression momentarily turning to one of concern as he eyed the youngster. Then the old man nodded at the camera he was holding, arched an eyebrow, and gestured with it in the teenager's direction.

Trey slowly put out a hand, and the old man thrust the device into it and nodded again, before moving over to stand next to an elderly Japanese woman who was waiting patiently by the wall with the ancient castle behind her.

'*Arigatou gozaimasu,*' the man said with one last quick bow.

Trey took their picture, handed the camera back and hurried off, suddenly feeling rather foolish but unable to shake the feeling of vulnerability. Perhaps heading out hadn't been such a great idea.

As he walked he mused over what had just happened. He couldn't go on like this, seeing everything and everyone around him as a potential threat. He wasn't even able to go out for a walk in the sunshine without believing he might be attacked. How was he supposed to live like this? How was he ever supposed to enjoy himself and behave in a way any normal teenager might? He let out a long sigh. That was the problem. Trey couldn't live like a normal fifteen-year-old because he wasn't one. And he never would be.

He was sick of it all. Almost everything he'd once considered normal was now totally screwed up. Even time was out of whack. When he'd left the human realm to go and find Alexa and Philippa in the Netherworld nobody had thought to explain to him that the two realms were temporally misaligned and that upon returning, months, not days, had elapsed. He'd missed his favourite band in concert, and he'd paid a fortune for those tickets. No wonder Philippa had opted to go and live in Lucien's luxury villa in the Seychelles for a year – she'd had enough of the madness too.

Back at the apartment everyone was discussing Caliban and his plans. Lucien's frustration at not being able to locate his brother had diffused through the place, and it seemed to Trey as if everyone was running around in a state of frantic disorder, trying to second-guess the vampire's next move. It used to be that the apartment was a sanctuary away from the day-to-day business of the downstairs offices, which policed the movement of nether-creatures between the two realms. But that had all gone out of the window since their return from the Netherworld, and now there was precious little time for anything else. Trey had come outside hoping to escape it all for a while, to relax a little, but his encounter with the Japanese tourist simply underlined how keyed up he was.

It wasn't just the activities back at the apartment that had Trey wound up, it was the reason behind them. The vampire Caliban was at large again, and if Lucien was right, he was somewhere in the human realm.

Trey squinted up at the sun once more. At least he was safe from attack by the psychopathic bloodsucker in the daylight. Of course, his minions were a different matter.

The teenager crossed the busy road, dodging the onrushing cars that blared their horns at him. He headed for the red, white and blue sign of Tower Hill station, thinking that he might take a tube train to Oxford Street. But at the last minute he veered away; the thought of pushing his way through the multitude of shoppers that would fill the busy streets there was the last thing he needed right now. Instead he turned towards the City, knowing that it would be quiet outside the working week.

His leg ached a little as he took a flight of stone steps down into a passage separating an ancient-looking church and a vast steel-and-glass office block. The wound he'd received at the Demon Games in the Netherworld was still a little tender, but it had healed exceptionally well and he knew that it was almost as good as new, despite the ugly scar that marked him now. He'd suffered a facial injury at the Games too, but if he were honest he rather liked the pink line of scar tissue that ran through his right eyebrow. It gave him a rough, tough look. The scars were permanent. Unlike the wounds he suffered at the hands of humans, the wounds inflicted on him by other nether-creatures did not heal in the same way.

He had no idea where he was going. He walked, turning left or right whenever it took his fancy, and pretty soon he was lost among the tall buildings and near-empty streets. He didn't mind. He kept his eyes fixed on the section of pavement immediately before him, the hood of his sweatshirt pulled up over his face to block out the outside world.

He stopped at a kerb and glanced up to check for cars despite the almost complete lack of traffic in this part of the city. A shop on the corner caught his eye. It was shut, the interior dark and uninviting, but the window packed full of comics and graphic novels looked interesting, so he approached it to take a look.

The lack of lighting inside the shop, coupled with the bright sunshine outside, made it difficult to see the display properly, and Trey was forced to make a visor out of his hands, curling them round his eyes and pressing them against the glass to get a proper look inside. He spotted a compilation book of one of his favourite Marvel characters, and he strained to see if it was one he already had or not. As he did so he got the uneasy feeling that he was being watched – a strange sixth sense that made the hairs on the back of his neck bristle and a cold shiver run through him. He turned round, looking to see if he could locate the source of the uneasiness.

There was nobody in sight.

Get a grip, Trey, he told himself, remembering his earlier overreaction to the tourist. But the uneasy sense of being watched would not leave him, and lately Trey had learned not to ignore his gut feelings.

He quickly walked off to his right, pulling his hood back from his head now, not wanting his peripheral vision restricted. He sped up, turning left, then right, and entering a narrow street with rows of garages on one side and ugly, squat business premises on the other. At the end of the road he could see an arch in a brick wall that looked as if it led into a children's playground; brightly painted swings and slides were just visible through the gap. In the background beyond this appeared to be a high-rise block of flats. That feeling of being followed was stronger than ever. Trey started running in the direction of the park, quickly lengthening his stride until he was sprinting. Doing his best to ignore the pain in his knee, he ate up the ground in front of him. He burst through the narrow brick archway, skidding to a halt as he did so and taking up position to one side of the opening. He quickly glanced about him, relieved to find that the playground was empty and that a line of tall trees at the far end obscured the view of most of the windows in the flats. At the last second he decided to remove his trousers and sweatshirt, kicking off his trainers too so that he stood there in nothing but his underwear, socks and a T-shirt.

Please God, don't let anyone look out now and see me standing in a children's play area in nothing but my pants!

It occurred to him that this could all be yet another episode of paranoia. He was losing it. He was imagining—

He stopped, holding his breath. Sure enough, Trey heard the sound of running footsteps approaching. That uneasy feeling he'd experienced at the bookshop was back, setting his nerves jangling and his heart thumping against his chest. He closed his eyes, praying that what he was about to do was the right thing.

He Changed.

The huge barrel-chested seven-foot werewolf that he now was crouched, and as his pursuer emerged through the bricked archway Trey threw himself forward, knocking whoever it was down to the ground. There was a loud 'Unfgh!' as they hit the small grassy mound on the other side of the opening. Trey was quickly on top of his quarry, pinning it down with his weight. He reached forward and pulled the hood back off its head.

But it was no demon beneath the hood. A pair of piercingly blue eyes stared out at him from behind a tangle of blonde hair.

Ella blew the hair away from her face, her annoyed expression quickly turning to amusement as she took in the astonished look on the werewolf's face.

'Hello, Trey,' she said.

When Trey had got over his shock at seeing Ella again, he pulled her back on to her feet. Growling an apology, he turned his back, returned to his human form and put his clothes back on. The ripped and ruined mess of his underwear and T-shirt were picked up and placed in a bin. Eventually he turned to look at Ella again and offered her an awkward smile.

'We should go somewhere and have a chat,' he suggested.

They found a little cafe where they could sit outside in the sunshine. He sat across the table from her, studying her as they waited for the waitress to fetch them their drinks. She was tall and attractive, with high cheekbones that made those penetrating blue eyes all the more startling. He remembered how, when they'd met for the first time in his Uncle Frank's house in Canada, he'd incorrectly suspected she wore coloured lenses. She had the same coloured eyes when she morphed into her white-furred werewolf form, which was unusual: most wolves lost their blue eyes as they grew from cubs to adults.

'What are you doing in London?' Trey asked.

Ella explained how her parents had refused to have anything more to do with her following her return from Canada. They reasoned that as she'd been stupid enough to run away with her playboy boyfriend there was no place for her back with them now that it had all gone wrong. She hadn't told them how she'd been lured there and deliberately

15

bitten by a werewolf pack's alpha leader, turning her into a lycanthrope too so that she had no choice but to stay there with him. How could she? She paused in her story with a sad smile and a shrug.

'But you know all about the Pack, and how it ended.' She gave him a strange look, pushing a strand of hair away from her eyes. When she continued it was in a lighter tone. 'So I decided to travel around Europe a bit and take in the sights. I found myself in London, remembered that you lived here, and made up my mind to track you down.'

There was something about her story that didn't quite ring true with Trey, but he dismissed the thought. He was glad to see her again, regardless of the truth behind why she was really here.

'So how did you find me?' he asked.

'I sensed you,' she said. She snorted a little and looked back at him with a puzzled expression. 'We're *werewolves*, Trey. Don't you *feel* it when there are others like us around?'

He frowned. 'No, I don't think I do. At least, not in the way you're suggesting. I think I sort of knew that you were around once you were close to me on the streets, but that's about it.' He shrugged. 'I guess I'm not your typical werewolf.'

There was a silence between them then. He realized she was staring at his sweatshirt, at the place where the talisman hung on a chain round his neck.

'Don't you miss it?' Ella said eventually.

'What?'

'The Pack. Don't you miss the feeling of . . . *togetherness*? Of belonging?'

Trey thought back to his time in Canada with the werewolf pack known as the LG78. He'd gone there to find his uncle, to try and come to terms with what he was and learn about his werewolf heritage. But instead his experiences had simply underlined the differences between him and other lycanthropes. He didn't fit in with the Pack. Because of the amulet he wore and because he was a true-blood werewolf – born of two, not one, lycanthrope parents – he would never be like them. He was different, and that difference had almost got him killed at the hands of the Pack leader, Jurgen. He looked at the girl sitting opposite him and smiled at her, remembering how she'd saved his life that day.

'I guess my experience of the Pack is slightly different from yours, Ella.'

She gave him that strange look again. 'Determined to be the lone wolf, is that it, Trey?'

She reached out for her coffee, and he caught a glimpse of the terrible scar on her arm that had resulted from her boyfriend's attack. The sight of it reminded him that she too was different. She hadn't been born a werewolf, and she'd also had to struggle to come to terms with what she'd become when she was deliberately bitten. He frowned, remembering that although his return from Canada still felt fairly recent, her own return had been some time ago and that at least three full moons must have come and gone for her. She had no amulet round her neck to control her transformations when the moon was at its fullest. And there was no Pack to look out for her now during the Change to make sure she didn't go off on some murderous rampage.

'How have you coped with your full moons since you've been back?' Trey asked.

She let the question hang in the air between them. Eventually she shook her head, smiled and changed the subject. 'Look, I've got some time in London, and I thought that maybe you and I could hang out?'

Trey frowned. He was about to tell her that he was a little busy right now, when he stopped. Hadn't he just that morning bemoaned the fact that he never got the chance to act like a normal teenager? Hadn't he wondered if he would ever be able to hang around with friends in the very way Ella was suggesting now?

'OK. Yeah, that'd be nice,' he said.

'Do you live near here?'

'Not far.'

'Great! Maybe you could show me your place?'

Trey thought about the apartment, and how it was teeming with nether-creatures right now. Not to mention Lucien, Tom – Lucien's right-hand man, Hag the witch and Alexa. His heart did a little bump when he thought of Alexa: he hadn't told her about Ella, and he wasn't sure how she'd react to him turning up with her. He glanced back at Ella, who was still smiling. He returned the smile.

'Yeah, sure. Why not?'

She stood up. 'Great. Let's go, shall we?'

'Now? You want to go right now?'

'Sure.' She caught the worried look on his face. 'Is now a bad time?'

Trey thought for a second before making up his mind. 'No, not really. I suppose now is as good a time as any.'

2

The drained, dead body of the woman remained on the floor where Caliban had dropped it earlier, and despite the cold, the ripe smell of death filled the room. He had considered simply pitching the corpse out of the window to let it fall and rot at the foot of the tower, but then another idea came to him, and using the simple spell she had taught him, he'd summoned the sorceress. They were alone in the huge tower, and he knew that she would be somewhere deep in its bowels. He had no intention of traipsing down there to find her, and he could imagine the way in which she would be cursing him right now as she made the long journey up to his rooms near the top. He'd once asked her why she didn't simply move about the place by magic, but she'd rolled her eyes and proceeded to lecture him on how needlessly difficult and draining that would be.

It was dark, although the vampire had little trouble seeing in the gloom, and his acute sense of hearing picked up the sorceress's approaching footsteps from way off. Eventually she knocked at the door, and the vampire smiled to himself, acknowledging her obedience to his earlier command. It was good to know that this ancient creature could be tamed.

It would not be easy, but the sorceress could be made to bend to his will.

'Come,' he said in a loud voice, taking up his position on the throne and facing the door as it opened.

'You summoned me?'

'Did I?' Caliban shook his head as if trying to remember why he might have done such a thing. 'Yes. Yes, I suppose I did.'

Helde waited. After a few moments it became clear that the vampire had no intention of carrying on.

'Well?' she said impatiently.

Caliban raised his metal prosthetic hand, and studied one of the bladed fingers as he flexed it in the air before him. 'Something has been bothering me, and I called you here so that you could put my mind at rest. After you left earlier, it occurred to me that it is foolish to wait any longer for you to demonstrate your powers to me.'

'I created the portal that got us here. A number of portals, in fact. I should have thought that you understood the great skill and—'

'Yes, yes,' Caliban said, waving his hand dismissively. 'But you know which powers I am referring to – those for which you were given your delightful moniker: Queen of the Dead.' Caliban stared across at her. 'It seems to me that your search for this "Shield" has distracted you from the real task in hand.' He paused for a moment. 'I, after all, went to a great deal of trouble to resurrect you, and I would not like to think that I went through all of that for nothing.'

'You doubt my abilities?'

The vampire flashed his fangs at the sorceress. 'Of course not. But you yourself had been dead for a very long time.' He narrowed his eyes in her direction. 'Let us just say that I am concerned your erstwhile skills may have become a little . . . rusty.' Caliban threw up his hands in a what-can-you-do gesture. 'And I've had bad experiences with reanimated undead creatures before!'

'You have nothing to worry about, Caliban. I can assure you—'

'Be that as it may,' the vampire interrupted again, 'I believe I would like to see what I can expect when we finally unleash your powers. So I think a small demonstration is in order.' He nodded towards the corpse. 'In your own time.'

There was a pause while Helde considered this. 'Do you realize how exhausting a reanimation is?'

'You can have a lie-down afterwards.' Caliban's eyes bored into the sorceress's.

Helde frowned, mumbling something under her breath that the vampire couldn't quite catch. Nevertheless, she walked over to the corpse, looking down at it as she did so. 'You'd better get the other human.'

'Which other human?' Caliban asked.

'Please do not play games with me, vampire. You captured *two* walkers when you went out hunting. This one and her partner. You will have to bring the other one out from wherever you are keeping him.'

'And why would I do that?'

She rolled her eyes, as if she were explaining all of this to a recalcitrant child. 'Zombies don't do much near fellow undead creatures like you and me.' She nodded towards the cadaver. 'They only react near the thing they prey upon – living humans – so if you really must insist on seeing what *that* will do once I reanimate it, you'd better have something around to pique its interest.'

'You expect me to give up my dinner?' Caliban said with mock indignation.

Helde shrugged. 'It's your idea to conduct this . . . *demonstration*. Besides, you assured me that you would keep your feeding to a minimum while we were here. I didn't expect you to start stockpiling your victims. We need to maintain a low profile, Caliban. It would not do to have to leave Leroth.'

'I take it that you have still not located this "Shield"?'

'Oh, I'll find it. Assuming, that is, I'm not interrupted every few minutes to perform parlour tricks for your entertainment.'

Caliban gave her a long, cold look which was met unblinkingly by the sorceress. Eventually he shrugged his shoulders and let out a long sigh. 'Very well. I will fetch the other human.'

'Not quite yet,' Helde said. 'Let's get this one ready first.'

The sorceress's body went rigid as she entered the trance-like state she'd told Caliban was necessary for her to perform the reanimation. Even the multitude of insects that made up her body seemed to slow their usual frenetic jostling. Her eyes were shut, but her lips moved almost imperceptibly, and the vampire could hear the slightest whisper of the long-forgotten, ancient words she uttered. It was an eerie sound, even to the vampire's ears. At irregular intervals the sorceress's body would suddenly spasm and jerk violently, as if a jolt of electricity had passed through it.

Caliban watched her from his throne. He was, in a way, attracted to the sorceress. He told himself that it was preposterous to think such a thing, but nevertheless, he found her alluring. He wondered if his recent behaviour – his baiting of her – had been as much a result of this attraction as his desire to bend her to his will.

There was another convulsion, this one even more violent than those before it, and Helde's eyes snapped open, staring into the middle distance before her. She opened her mouth and issued a harsh hissing sound, like the noise of a retreating wave on a pebble beach. It went on for an impossible length of time, as if the breath were no longer the sorceress's but was coming from some other source outside her body. At the same time a small contingent of insects detached itself from Helde, falling to the floor and scurrying off in the direction of the corpse. The insects crawled into the mouth and nostrils of the dead body, burrowing their way inside the cavities before disappearing.

Nothing happened for a while. That incessant hiss still came out of Helde's mouth, and just as Caliban was about to say something he saw, out of the corner of his eye, the body of the dead human buck into the air. Like the spasms that had racked the sorceress, it was a sudden and violent paroxysm, making the corpse's arms and legs fly out on all sides, leaving it face down and spreadeagled on the floor. The ghastly noise that the sorceress had been making finally came to an abrupt halt, only to be replaced by a low and terrible groaning from the creature on the floor.

The zombie raised its head and slowly pulled its arms underneath it to push itself up. Each and every movement was accompanied by a low groan. With a great effort the creature got to its knees, then feet, until it stood facing the vampire and sorceress, swaying a little on the spot as though it might topple forward at any moment.

Caliban looked from the zombie to Helde. The sorceress appeared to be exhausted, her head lolling as if she lacked the strength to even lift it.

'Make it do something,' he said. He was excited to see what his new weapon, the one that would be unleashed in the first wave of the forthcoming war on the humans, was capable of.

Helde slowly lifted her eyes to meet his. She waved an arm in the direction of the door. 'Bring the other one in,' she said.

The male was being kept in the room next door. Caliban hissed angrily – he was used to giving orders, not taking them – but one look at Helde told him she was probably incapable of fetching anything herself.

The human was in the same position the vampire had

placed him in when he had brought the pair back to the tower. Caliban had spellbound the man: a useful ability that all vampires possess to keep their prey docile and obedient.

'Follow me,' the vampire said.

They paused before the doors leading back into the room containing the sorceress and the revenant.

'Look at me,' the vampire demanded, nodding as the human raised his head.

'In a moment you and I will walk through these doors. You will remain under my influence until they are closed behind you. As soon as they are shut, my control over you will cease except for one thing: you will not know that I, or anyone else *except* the woman you were with when I captured you, is in the room. Do you understand me?'

'Yes.'

'Good.'

The vampire opened the doors and stepped inside. He walked over to the sorceress and took her by the arm, guiding her to a corner cloaked in shadows from which they could watch. Satisfied with the set-up, he turned back to fetch the human, ushering the man ahead of him and placing him a little way inside the room, facing the creature by the window. Caliban looked about him. Everything was in place, so he reached out and pushed the doors shut.

The sound of the door closing woke the human from the stupor he was in. He shook his head from side to side, as if trying to wake from a particularly disturbing dream. When he lifted his face, he gasped at the sight of his girlfriend wavering on the spot before him. What meagre light there was came in through the window at her back, casting her features into shadow and rendering it impossible for him to make out her face.

'Anna?' he said.

The darkness was of no consequence to the vampire. His eyes scanned the man's face, and it was clear that the latter sensed something was wrong with his erstwhile lover. The vampire leaned forward in anticipation.

When the man spoke again, it was in an urgent whisper, the panic in his voice clear to hear. 'We need to get out of here. We need to go, now. We've got to get away from that creature that brought us here.' He sniffed the air, looking about him. 'What's that terrible smell?'

There was a low groan from the zombie, and the man froze at the strange sound.

'Anna?' the man said again, taking another step forward to try and get a better look at the thing before him.

The zombie, which had stood unmoving throughout, suddenly exploded into action. A terrible high-pitched shriek came from its mouth as it leaped forward, snaking out an arm to grab the man round the back of his neck and yanking him forward, so that he stumbled and lost his footing. He went down on one knee, and looked up just in time to see the thing as it attacked him, the long black hair on the zombie's head whipping back and forth as it set about its helpless victim. It curled its fingers into vicious hooks that it used to grab both sides of the man's head, lowering its face to meet his. But there was no lover's kiss at the end of this deadly embrace. The man screamed his former lover's name as the zombie dipped its head and sank its teeth into his cheek, pulling away and chewing on a gory clod of flesh.

The man's agonized shrieks echoed around the stone walls of the room, and he fell backwards, hands clutching the side of his face in an effort to staunch the river of crimson that poured from the wound. The zombie set about him again, this time going for the throat, ignoring the defensive kicks and blows that the man aimed back at it. A moment or so later, the human's screams were cut off forever.

Caliban watched as the zombie straightened up. It was covered in gore now, and it chewed on whatever it had in its mouth before swallowing. It looked down at the dead body beneath it, its face expressionless – the fury that had consumed it seconds before had disappeared as quickly as it had ignited. It appeared completely uninterested in the body now that the man was dead.

The smell of hot blood was almost too much for the vampire. He turned to look at the sorceress at his side who was still wavering on the spot like a drunkard.

'They move much faster than I would have imagined.'

'The fresh ones do. Those that have been in the ground for any length of time are not so quick.'

Caliban glanced back at the zombie, which was now sitting beside its victim, staring straight ahead unseeingly.

'Why does it not continue to feed?' he asked.

'The dead body no longer has any appeal. The zombie seeks only to kill the living, as if it seeks to steal back the thing it once had. It doesn't need to eat to survive, and once it has dispatched its victim, it quickly loses interest. If there were other living humans here now it would move on to them, continuing to kill until they were all dead or it was stopped in some way.'

'And what of the victim?'

Helde glanced at the dead body on the ground beside the zombie. 'He is infected now. In a short time he will awaken as a zombie himself.'

'Infected?'

She nodded. 'Even if he had not been killed, the bite to his face would have been enough to ensure that he would become undead. He'd have become very ill first: fever, hallucinations, fits and eventual "death". But he would reanimate a short while after.'

'And that's how they spread. Infecting others around them like a virus,' Caliban said, nodding to himself as he thought about releasing creatures like these into the human realm.

'As long as I am alive, yes.'

'What?'

'The infection has been created through sorcery. Through dark magic. I created it, and it exists because of me. If you were to kill me now, the female zombie would survive as a zombie – she has already *turned* – but the infected one would stay dead and not zombify. If she had not finished him off by savaging his neck in that way, and he'd simply become sick as a result of that first bite, he could fully recover if I, and the zombification sorcery, were to die.'

He looked at her as he took this in. 'That is interesting,' he said.

'I need to rest,' the sorceress said.

'Of course.'

'It will be many hours before I am able to function properly again.'

'*Hours?*' The vampire looked at her in horror.

'I told you that the process of reanimation was exhausting for me.'

Another thought occurred to Caliban. 'How many zombies do you think you could create in a day? The maximum number?'

'Two or three.'

He stared at her for a long time, his face becoming a mask of anger and disbelief. 'And how are we to create a zombie army if the best you can do is two or three at a go!'

'And I would need at least that many days to recover in between.'

'You have deceived me, sorceress!' he said, taking a step towards her.

'No,' she said, her hands coming up before her as she backed off. 'It was never my intention to use my sorcery

30

skills to create zombie after zombie for you, Caliban. Why would I?' She gestured towards the revenant and the dead body beside it. 'You yourself compared them to a virus which spreads. We already have one zombie, and another on the way. All we need to do is capture as many humans as we can, and unleash these two among them. Before you know it, we will have the beginnings of our army. Once we release enough of them in the human realm, the numbers will grow exponentially.'

Caliban considered this. Eventually he nodded.

'Good. Then I suggest you get that rest you need, because tomorrow we will begin to create our undead army.'

3

Alexa stepped into the elevator and pressed the button for the top floor and the apartment. The various bags that she'd accumulated during her afternoon shopping trip nudged and jostled at her knees, and she glanced down at them, giving a small sigh. It seemed that even shopping wasn't enough to lift her spirits any more. She smiled briefly as she caught sight of the Selfridges bag among her other things: in it were a pair of three-quarter-length khaki shorts she'd bought for Trey, hoping that they'd cheer him up a bit. He'd been so withdrawn lately, staying in his room and avoiding everyone. And when she asked Tom if he thought she should say something, he'd advised her not to, reasoning that Trey was simply convalescing from his injuries, and would be back to his old self in no time. She'd gone along with him, but hadn't revealed that she thought there might be more to it than that, and that *she* was the person Trey was trying to avoid, embarrassed by the things they'd said to each other about their feelings when they were captives of the demon lord, Molok.

The elevator slowed to a halt and the doors slid apart.

The first thing that greeted Alexa was the sound of laughter: Trey's laughter. The sound lightened her mood considerably, and she wondered briefly if Tom might not have been correct after all. He was playing music too. She stepped out of the lift on to the deep carpet, faltering when she saw the blonde-haired stranger sitting next to Trey on the leather couch. They had their backs to her, and the music was loud enough to cover the sound of her entry.

Blondie leaned in towards Trey, who was pointing something out to her in a magazine he was holding. She nudged him playfully with her head, said something and burst out laughing. Alexa couldn't believe how strongly the girl was coming on to Trey, who seemed oblivious to her advances, too dense to pick up on the signals. Alexa watched Blondie push a stray lock of hair away from her face, smiling at Trey as she did so.

'Hello,' Alexa said in a loud voice.

Trey jumped up off the couch and turned to face her. He blushed, looking like a child caught with his hand in the cookie jar just before dinnertime.

'Lex . . . er . . . hi.' He waved at her, a clumsy and awkward greeting. 'This . . . this is Ella. She's a friend of mine.' He gestured in Blondie's direction, and the girl stood up next to him, giving Alexa a little nod.

'Nice to meet you, Ella,' Alexa said, returning the nod and moving off in the direction of the kitchen. 'Don't let me stop you two having fun,' she said as she passed.

Trey noted the strained tone with which Alexa had spoken, and he watched her as she stiffly walked the length of the room to enter the kitchen without so much as another glance in his direction.

He looked from the kitchen doorway to the girl standing at his side and then back again, as if trying to make up his mind what to do next. 'I won't be a minute,' he said to Ella, pointing in the direction of the kitchen before moving off towards it.

He entered the room and closed the door behind him.

'What's up?' he asked.

'Up?'

'Yeah. And don't tell me nothing's up because it is.'

'What could possibly be up?' Alexa said, turning away from him and putting her shopping bags on the side.

Trey stayed quiet and waited.

She went over to the fridge and took out a bottle of water, opened it and took a swig. When she turned back, she raised her eyebrows, feigning surprise to find him still standing there. She pulled the bottle from her lips. 'Shouldn't you be out there entertaining your *guest*?'

Trey looked at her for a minute, a frown beetling his brow, and suddenly his expression changed to one of annoyance. 'Is that what this is about? The fact that I've invited a friend over?'

'Why should I have a problem with that?'

'You tell me.'

There was another brief silence, and when Alexa spoke again, her voice was low and quiet.

'Who is she?' she asked.

'We met in Canada. She's a lycanthrope. A Bitten. She saved my life.'

Alexa looked as if all of the stuffing had suddenly been pulled from her. She gave Trey an incredulous look, her mouth open in a little oh.

'She saved your life?'

'Yes.'

Alexa let out a short derisive snort and shook her head. 'I can't believe you sometimes.'

'What?'

'How come you've never told me about her, hmm? How come I know nothing about this girl who *saved your life* until I walk into this apartment to find you sitting with her on the couch giggling away together like a couple of . . . idontknowwhats?'

'In case you hadn't noticed, you and I haven't exactly had a great deal of time for each other since we got back. This place—'

'And whose fault is that, hmm? Whose fault is it that we've hardly said more than a few words to each other since coming back?' She paused briefly. 'You've been avoiding me, Trey!'

'That's ridiculous.'

'Is it? Then how do you explain that every time I walk into a room, you find some excuse to walk out again. How is it that if I'm in the living room, you stay in your room and only come out once I've gone. Don't deny it, Trey, because if there's one thing you are not, it's a good liar.'

She stared at him, her jaw pushed forward, lips pressed together, eyes wide as if daring him to contradict her.

'Look—'

'No, you look,' she interrupted angrily. She stopped and took a deep breath, pulling herself together. When she spoke next, her voice was softer. 'I don't want you to feel that you owe me anything. When we were in the Netherworld you and I said things about the way we felt towards each other. You came to rescue me, Trey, and I'll never forget that. But in times of immense pressure people do, and say, strange things.' She smiled sadly. 'I suppose what I'm trying to tell you is that I don't want the things we said . . . to come between us. Let's put it down to the stress we were both under, eh? If we can do that, hopefully we can go back to the way things were before and not feel uncomfortable around each other.'

Trey stood looking back at her, unable or unwilling to say anything for a moment or two. Eventually he shook his head and blew out his cheeks. 'You're saying you didn't mean any of those things, is that right?'

'I'm saying that perhaps we were both a bit . . . rash.'

She looked up to see the muscles at the side of Trey's jaw bunching and unbunching as if he were desperately trying to contain himself.

'Fine, if that's the way you want it,' he said.

'Don't you?'

He bit his bottom lip, and was about to say something

else when he obviously thought better of it. Nodding his head stiffly at her, he turned and left the room.

Alexa looked across at the worktop where she'd thrown her shopping and spotted the bag containing the shorts she'd bought for Trey. She wasn't quite expecting the tears that quickly came to her eyes and rolled down her cheeks.

Ten minutes later, when she'd calmed down and washed her face, she went out into the living room again. Trey and Ella had left.

4

Tom opened the door and stepped out on to the roof of the building, glancing across at the chrome-and-glass construction that housed the swimming pool as he did so. The pool was rarely used, and he could usually guarantee that he would be alone up here when he needed to think. He was tense. He'd been working all morning to try and locate where Caliban and Helde might have gone when they disappeared from the Netherworld, but had had no luck. When he detected movement out of the corner of his eye he spun round, crouching slightly, his hand already reaching inside his jacket for the semi-automatic pistol in its shoulder holster.

Trey had looked back over his shoulder at the sound of the door opening. He noted how frazzled his friend looked, and it struck him as strange – except for Lucien, Tom was the most level-headed and unflappable person he knew. He nodded his head at the Irishman, and turned back to look out over the London skyline.

Tom hesitated for a moment before walking over to stand beside the boy. The two of them studied the vista in silence for a while.

'Nice up here, isn't it?' the Irishman said eventually.

'Yeah. It's peaceful.'

The two shared another long silence. 'You OK?' Tom finally said.

Trey shrugged noncommittally. 'I suppose so.'

'A penny for your thoughts, young man.'

'I was just wondering when it'll all end,' Trey said. He turned his attention to the Canary Wharf tower and the other tall buildings which surrounded it. 'When all of this *madness* that's become my life will finally stop. Is it too much to ask? To wish for a life that doesn't involve looking over my shoulder all of the time in case a murderous vampire or one of his cohorts is creeping up on me? A life that's just a bit more . . . *normal*?'

The Irishman shook his head and sighed. 'You're not wrong to want that, lad. And no, it's not too much to ask.' He thought about everything that had happened to Trey in the short time that he'd known him, since Lucien – an old friend of Trey's father – had invited him into their lives and world. In particular, he thought about the boy's recent exploits in Canada, where he'd gone with such high hopes of finding a family member who would help him cope with his lycanthropy. Instead, he'd found his Uncle Frank: a bitter and twisted drunk who'd wanted nothing to do with the boy.

And then there had been the Netherworld and Trey's forced participation in the vicious and twisted Demon Games to win freedom for himself and Alexa.

Nobody should have to go through such things –

particularly one so young. Tom drummed his fingertips against the top of the metal rail. He thought the world of the boy, and he wished he could tell him that everything was going to be all right, but in truth, he wasn't sure it was.

'I think things are coming to a head,' Tom said instead. He let the statement hang in the air for a moment before continuing. 'Caliban has almost complete control of the Netherworld, and we know he's planning something big here in the human realm. One way or another, this thing will end soon.'

Trey nodded. 'Don't you ever feel like just walking out on it all? You could, you know. No one would blame you if you just upped and left all this . . .' he gestured with his hands in the air before him, '. . . this *madness* to the nether-creatures. It's not really your fight, Tom.' He stopped and shook his head, still staring out ahead of him, before adding, 'I'm not even certain that it's mine.'

They stood there, comfortable enough in each other's company not to feel the need to fill the ensuing silence with pointless small talk.

Tom eventually broke the silence, speaking in a low, quiet voice that made Trey turn to look at him.

'The answer to your question is no. I wouldn't walk away from it all. Oh, don't get me wrong, I have a hard time dealing with a lot of the things I come across, and I often crave a bit of normality over all the "paranormality", but whenever it gets too much for me I remember how close I was to death when Lucien saved me from those bloodsucking freaks. Not only that, Lucien is a friend of mine, just as you and Alexa are, and I'd never walk out on my friends.'

'Alexa and I had a row.' Trey said after a moment.

In spite of himself, Tom couldn't help but smile at this last revelation.

'Does this *normal* life that you want so much mean that you can't have a girlfriend who's a dhampir sorceress?' Tom said.

'It would seem it does.'

'That sucks.'

'Yeah.'

A cloud passed across the sun, and the two of them watched as its shadow rolled over the buildings and streets of the capital.

'But you know, there's no such thing as a normal life, Trey. Things have a habit of getting in the way of us leading the lives that we *think* we'd like. And anyhow, normality's overrated.'

The sun came out again, and Trey looked across at his friend. 'What did I do before I had you to talk sense to me, Tom?' he said, half playfully.

'Oh, I suspect you worked things out for yourself. It probably just took a little bit longer.' He winked in the boy's direction.

Trey smiled at the big Irishman and moved towards the exit. 'Thanks for the chat, Tom,' he said, reaching for the door.

Tom nodded and waved at the boy, watching him as he disappeared through the opening, before turning about again and leaning against the guardrail. He was worried about the youngster, and he determined to talk to Lucien about his concerns.

5

Lucien glanced at the small clock on his desk. There was an hour to go before the meeting he'd called with the others to discuss updated strategies for finding his brother, a goal he knew they were no closer to achieving as of this morning, despite all their best efforts. He was feeling tired and more than a little cranky, no doubt as a result of not having fed for two days. His eyes rested for a moment on the wooden panel behind which was concealed a small fridge with the bags of fresh blood that had been delivered by courier that morning. He should feed before the meeting. He steepled his hands in front of him and rested his forehead against the fingertips, closing his eyes for a second.

When he opened them again it was to darkness.

He lay in a stone casket, the cold of its walls radiating back through his own frigid flesh. The heavy lid was pulled across, plunging the interior into complete darkness. He stirred, aware that something was wrong but unable to determine what it was. He opened his eyes, looking up into the void that surrounded him and trying to ascertain what could have summoned him from his sleep. There were no sounds from the room outside, and his senses told him that there was nobody there.

He reached up and hooked his fingers into the recesses on the underside of the lid, pushing against it and ignoring the loud, grating sound it made as it slid aside. He slowly sat up and looked around. The feeling of unease and danger refused to go.

Caliban hissed, turning his head to look out of the window at the grey, swirling mist that marked the boundary between the two worlds. He considered calling Helde when—

Lucien opened his eyes again, his head reeling from the vision he'd just seen. He stood up, ignoring the helter-skelter sensation that the sudden movement produced. He had experienced something like this once before – when his brother had escaped from the Netherworld after reviving the sorceress Helde. Then, as now, the vicarious experience of looking out through his brother's eyes and sharing his thoughts had left him feeling sick and disorientated.

His brother might have been alerted to his presence before he broke the connection. He hoped not. He glanced again at the antique timepiece in front of him, grabbed the phone and called Tom, telling him to get everyone assembled for the meeting *now* and that he'd be downstairs in no more than five minutes. When he disconnected from the call he smiled for the first time in days.

He knew where his brother and the sorceress were hiding.

6

There were six of them in total. Hag had been the last to arrive, but now she, Trey, Tom, Alexa and two senior members of Lucien's staff sat on one side of the table in one of the large meeting rooms downstairs, looking across at the empty seat opposite them. Despite their questions, all the Irishman could tell them was that Lucien had important news to share.

Alexa had arrived just before the old sorceress, walking straight past her usual seat on Trey's left and taking one at the other end of the table, putting Tom and the others between them. As she passed him he'd turned his head and nodded at her, but she'd ignored him, sitting down and fixing her gaze on the table instead.

Hag's entrance had been far from quiet. The old woman, who had returned to the human realm with them after Trey's adventures in the Demon Games, had burst into the room, shouting and cursing at the vast tree-like mandragore she'd ordered to stay outside. The huge creature stood on the other side of the doorway, its enormous bulk blocking out everything behind it. The creature was the thing of nightmares. A cruel, ancient looking face – deep-set black eyes above a horizontal slash that served as a mouth – was set into the top of the 'trunk' body which was a vast bloated version of the bulbous root the thing had been grown from. Thick, muscular limbs hung down, and these, like the rest of the creature, were covered in coarse, bark-like skin. Clumsy and cumbersome, the creature shuffled around after the sorceress everywhere she went, an imposing bodyguard whose scream had once been deadly, killing every living thing in the vicinity of the noise, until Hag had had her sentinel's voice removed.

'Did you *have* to bring that thing with you?' Tom asked the sorceress.

The mandragore narrowed its eyes at Tom, opening its mouth wide in a threatening gesture.

Hag tutted in the creature's direction. 'Hush. The silly fool of a man didn't mean to be rude. Did you?' She raised her eyebrows at Tom, but got a withering look in response. Hag turned once more to the creature as if it were a naughty child, and indeed in many ways it *was* like a child to her; she had raised the thing from a root, feeding it blood and milk and honey until it became the terrible thing now in the doorway. 'Just stop sulking and wait for me there,' she said, slamming the door on the creature's face.

She took a seat, rolling her eyes at those already sitting round the table. 'I wanted to leave it in the Netherworld, but it made such a fuss that I had to bring it along with me.'

46

Moments later Lucien appeared. Moving briskly, he took up a seat at the centre of one side of the oval table so that he could see, and be seen by, everyone.

'Thank you for coming. I won't keep you long,' he said, glancing around him for the first time. 'I think . . .' He began, then stopped and shook his head a little. 'No, I *know* where my brother is hiding.'

'And how do you know this?' Hag said. 'Have you had a tip-off, because I'd be very wary of—'

The vampire held a hand up to stop her. 'A short while ago, I had another of those strange episodes. Like the one I had when Caliban was escaping the Netherworld. It was as if I were looking through his eyes and experiencing his thoughts.' He paused, frowning now. 'I don't seem to have any control over when these "visions" will occur. They are something new to me, but they could be very useful.'

Hag pursed her lips and nodded, as if she had no problem accepting this. Nevertheless, the strange look she gave him at the same time unsettled the vampire. Since being brought back from the dead a second time by Trey and his daughter, after Caliban had attacked and poisoned him, Lucien had found himself experiencing changes. In many ways he had seemed to be reverting to the vampire self he had so carefully erased as part of his fight against the Netherworld – fangs regrowing, his appetite for blood still under control but much, much stronger. But when they were in the Netherworld together Hag had alluded to more significant alterations to come. He had chosen to ignore her. He still did.

'Where is he?' Alexa said.

'In Leroth.'

There was a long silence, during which Alexa glanced in Trey's direction for the first time; he was the one staring at the table now, his face suddenly pale upon hearing this news.

The Tower of Leroth was where Trey had killed Gwendolin, Alexa's mother, while defending himself and their friend Charles from the sorceress. The two of them had only spoken once about this, and although Alexa had never indicated that she blamed him for what happened, she knew that Trey had seen and done terrible things there – things which still haunted him.

'Oh,' she said.

Lucien nodded in response. 'I take it we do not have anyone watching the place, Tom?'

'That's right. With the death of Gwendolin, we assumed the tower had been abandoned by Caliban. She was thought to be the only person capable of translocating the place and so making it useful to him.' He hissed through his teeth. 'I'm sorry, Lucien, I should have—'

The vampire halted his friend with a shake of his head. 'You were not to know. And you are not to blame. I should have foreseen this when Caliban and Helde escaped the Netherworld. They would need somewhere to hide. What better place than Leroth?'

'And you think it's still in Iceland?' Alexa asked.

The vampire nodded. 'That is the impression I got from the brief time I was inside my brother's head.'

'Helde could move the tower,' Hag said. 'The question is, why hasn't she done so already? Why leave it where it was?'

'Exactly *because* they know we have not been keeping an eye on it.' Tom suggested. 'If the tower moves, they run the risk of being discovered.'

'Or,' Hag said, frowning as she ran through the possibilities in her mind, 'because she's been too preoccupied with something else.'

'Nursing Caliban back to health?' Tom suggested. 'We know he was in a bad way when they escaped.'

'He was fine,' Lucien said. 'My brother is back to full strength.'

'So she's doing something else,' Alexa mused. 'Something that she needed to be at Leroth for.'

Everybody considered this for a moment.

'The Shield,' Hag said. 'She's looking for the Shield.'

'What Shield?' Tom asked.

'When Leroth was used by Skaleb to defeat his brother in the Demon Wars, it was not just the tower's relocation powers that were key to his victory. The tower was said to have had a powerful Shield that could be employed to protect it. Like a great domed force field that spread out around it, stopping anything getting in or out.'

'And why would Helde and my brother want such a thing?'

'As I told you before, Lucien, Helde is a great sorceress, and she has a particular proclivity for . . . raising the dead.' Hag paused. 'And what better place to grow a zombie army? What better place to start your war against the human world?'

'How far around the tower could this Shield extend?' Lucien asked.

'That would depend on the skill and power of the sorceress holding it in place,' Hag replied.

A silence hung over the room as they considered what the old woman had just said.

Trey stood up, his chair tipping backwards and hitting the floor with a loud thud, causing the others to turn and look at the teenager. It was obvious to everyone how upset he was; the muscles at the sides of his jaw were bunched and his eyes had a hard, steely look to them.

'Trey?' Lucien said, realizing that the teenager had not said a word since the location of Caliban had been revealed.

Without so much as a backward glance, Trey turned and left the room.

Lucien and Tom exchanged a look. Then the vampire took a deep breath and gazed about him at the remaining faces. 'I have contacted our people in Iceland, and they are on their way to Leroth as we speak. If my hunch is right and my brother was aware of me as I visited his mind, I think we'll be too late and Helde will have moved the tower before our people get there.

'What I need you and every other person in this organization to do now is to find where she moves Leroth to. There is nothing with a greater priority right now. Is that understood?' They nodded back at him. 'Very well, I suggest you go and start work.'

'I'd appreciate a quick word with you,' Tom said, staying in his seat.

Lucien nodded.

'You need to talk to the boy,' Tom said as soon as the room was clear.

'Is there something wrong?'

Tom snorted. 'Beside the fact that he's terrified he's about to meet his end at the hands of your nefarious brother? No, nothing's wrong at all.' The Irishman frowned. 'He's not the same person that left for the Netherworld. He's . . . different. We had a chat earlier and he asked me why I'd never walked away from all this.' He gestured towards the busy office behind him on the other side of the door. 'He said that it wasn't really my fight, and . . . well, he suggested that maybe it wasn't his either.'

The vampire nodded, a sad look on his face. 'Sometimes it's easy to forget he's just a young boy.'

'I got the impression *he* was on the verge of walking away.'

'I'll talk to him. Get him to see that he's safer here with us than anywhere else.'

'That's grand,' Tom said, getting up from his chair.

'Why haven't you? Why haven't you walked away from all this?'

'Ah, you know me. There's nothing I like more than a good punch-up. Besides, who'd look after you if I weren't around?'

'Who indeed?' Lucien said. He was about to say something else when he was interrupted by Hag bursting back into the room without so much as a knock.

'I need you to come with me,' she said to Lucien. 'Upstairs to your apartment. I want to try something, and I need you to help me do it.'

'And this can't wait?'

'Well, yes, it *could*. But I don't see why it should. We've all put it off for long enough.' And she rushed off without another word of explanation.

The elevator slowed to a halt, a soft pinging sound announcing their arrival at the penthouse apartment on the top floor. The doors slid open to reveal the splendour of the place.

The mandragore was already waiting for them. They'd had to send it up in the lift ahead: the huge weight and size of the man-tree thing was nearly too much for the machinery, and they'd had to virtually fold the creature in two to get it into the elevator car.

Hag strode out ahead of Lucien and Tom, the mandragore turning and joining the rear of the group. The old woman

52

moved deceptively quickly as she made her way to the far end of the room, turning right into the kitchen. The light in the place was dazzling, the late morning sunshine pouring in through the wall of glass that made up one side of the space.

Hag moved towards the balcony doors. 'Hold him and bring him here,' she shouted over her shoulder.

The mandragore reached out and wrapped one wooden arm round Lucien's neck, the other around his middle, pulling the vampire in towards it in a vice-like grip and stepping into the kitchen.

Several things then happened at once.

Hag reached out as if to open the sliding doors that made up the wall of glass.

Tom was the first to react, pulling the 9mm Glock 17 pistol out of the holster and aiming it at the mandragore. Realizing that the gun would have no chance of harming such a formidable creature, the Irishman quickly swung the weapon about and trained the forward sight on the centre of the old woman's forehead.

'I don't know what you're playing at, witch, but you'd better tell that walking log to let him go!' the Irishman demanded. 'And step away from those windows, or I'll blow your ugly old head clean off your shoulders.'

The old woman smiled at him sweetly, showing him a mouthful of ruined teeth.

Lucien tried to 'mist'. Like all vampires he had the ability to disappear and reappear instantaneously a short distance away. He attempted to do this now, but something was wrong. Something was stopping him misting out of the mandragore's clutches. He glanced at Hag, and knew from the look that she shot him that she was somehow blocking his ability to escape in this way.

'Let him go!' Tom demanded. 'I'll not ask again!'

'Or you'll do what?' Hag said, frowning. 'Fire your water pistol at me?'

Something was happening to the gun in Tom's hand. The Glock has a plastic polymer body, and because of this can be used in extreme temperatures, where traditional metal-bodied guns might fail. But the weapon in Tom's hand felt for all the world like it was made out of frozen steel. He took his eyes off his target for a second and glanced at the firearm. The gun had changed in appearance too. The dull, grey exterior had disappeared and the pistol had become transparent. Tom pulled the trigger, which snapped off under the pressure. He was holding a gun made of nothing but ice.

Hag turned towards the glass doors again.

'NO!' Tom shouted. He tried to run towards her but his feet wouldn't move. He looked about him in panic, searching for something he could use as a weapon, something he could hurl at the sorceress to stop her from doing what she was about to do.

'Stop! For heaven's sake! Don't do it!' Tom roared.

The old woman slid back one of the huge glass panels, and the sun's rays hit Lucien, bathing him in fiery light.

'NO!' Tom roared.

That much direct sunlight should have killed the vampire. His skin should have boiled and blistered, turning black as it did so. Smoke and the smell of ancient burning flesh should have filled the room as he writhed about in a torment of agony. That much sunshine should have killed him within seconds.

Lucien slowly opened his eyes and looked at the glowing sphere. It was the first time in over two hundred years that he had felt the warmth of the life-giving sun directly on his long dead skin without it instantly burning and blistering. He had never imagined that he could experience it again, and the emotions that this epiphany stirred up inside him were overwhelming. He was filled with the greatest elation he had experienced since witnessing the birth of his daughter, and try as he might, he could not fight the torrent of feeling that swept over him. He stood in the sun and allowed blood-red tears to roll from his eyes and down his cheeks.

'What? What the hell –?' Tom stuttered. He looked down and realized that he could move again. The pistol in his hand had returned to its true state, sans trigger, which lay on the floor at his feet.

He looked across at Lucien, who was staring back at Hag with a blood-streaked look of utter astonishment.

'How did you know?' Tom asked the sorceress.

'A hunch.'

'A hunch!'

The old woman looked at him and shrugged her shoulders. 'It was a good hunch though, wasn't it?' She turned to

55

face the vampire. 'I told you that you'd changed, Lucien. I told you that you were unique. A twice undead creature. A vampire that can walk in the sun! I told you that back in the Netherworld, but you didn't believe me.' She nodded at the mandragore, and the creature let go of the vampire. 'These *visions* you're having are also a result of this change.'

Lucien turned to the Irishman now. He removed a handkerchief from his pocket and wiped at the bloody tracks on his face, turning the white cotton square into a grisly scarlet mess. He seemed incapable of speech or action, something that Tom had never before seen in his friend. Eventually he seemed to gather himself together, and when he spoke it was to all of them.

'I wonder if you could all please leave me alone for a while? I need some time to think.'

7

'I've found it!' Helde shouted, throwing the doors open and bursting into the room at the top of the tower.

The silence she met reminded her that she ought to have knocked, but if Caliban was annoyed about her sudden entrance he didn't show it. Indeed, there was no reaction at all from the vampire. He remained sitting motionless on his throne, staring straight ahead of him, as if unaware that she'd even come in. The two zombies were in the room, the female sitting on the stone floor, hunched over, her back to the sorceress. The other, the man, was standing by the window. He briefly flicked his eyes at Helde and let out a low moan before staring blankly ahead again.

'Did you hear me?' she said. 'I've found the source of the Shield.'

The vampire cast his eyes towards her. He frowned as if confused as to who she was and what she might be doing here.

Helde looked about her, trying to locate the source of whatever had caused this strange impassivity in the vampire.

'My brother,' Caliban said. 'He knows where we are.'
'What? How?'

'It would appear that he really can see through my eyes when I am least expecting it.' He threw his hands into the air and spat.

'When did this happen?' she asked.

'A short while ago. I was awoken from my rest by something. I got up and looked around, but there was nothing, at least no threat that I could make out. Then very slowly I *felt* him. He was inside me, looking out through my eyes and sharing my thoughts. It's the same thing I felt just before we left the Netherworld.' His voice was getting louder now. 'What is happening to me, sorceress? How can he be capable of this thing?' He brought his fist down on to the stone arm of the throne with such force that the obsidian broke beneath the impact, a large piece of the polished black stone falling to the floor with a *thunk*. The vampire was on his feet and glaring down at her from the raised dais, as if the incident were somehow her fault.

She held out her hands in a pacifying gesturing, nodding with her head for him to sit again. She had already been a victim of the vampire's brutality, and she was keen to have him calm down as soon as possible lest he should take his frustrations out on her.

'Why didn't you call me?' she asked.

'I . . . don't know. At first I thought that I might have imagined the whole affair, but now I'm certain that that is not the case. He was *here,*' he tapped at his temple with a bony finger, 'inside my head!'

'Before the incident in the Netherworld, had either of you experienced any psychic or telepathic exchanges between each other?'

'Never.'

'You're sure?'

The vampire hissed and glared at her. 'That is not how it works between vampires. Humans, yes.' He took a deep breath and carried on. 'We have the ability to briefly "look inside" a human's thoughts and memories, but that power does not extend to our own kind.' He paused. 'And this was not like that. This was an altogether different thing. It was like he'd crawled inside me, like we were sharing the same body.'

The sorceress was quiet for a while as she considered what she'd just been told. 'I'll consult the ancient texts in the libraries here, to see if I can find any mention of such a thing.' She looked towards the zombies, another thought striking her. 'It puts a new light on our plans.'

'We will have to move the tower, take it to a new location where we can harvest humans and—'

'And what if your brother visits you again? And again? How much time will we waste moving here and there, achieving nothing?'

The vampire bellowed in frustration, the zombies briefly raising their heads at the sound.

The sorceress had never seen him so volatile. She watched him pace back and forth on the raised dais, muttering to himself in a low voice. It was odd to witness this ancient creature, normally so sure of his powers and ability, battling with these new, unwelcome emotions.

'We must alter our plans. Act faster.' She looked at him and nodded her head. 'Now perhaps you will understand why I have spent so much effort searching for the Shield. My search could not have ended at a more opportune time.'

'You have found it?'

'That is what I came here to tell you.'

'How must we change our plans?'

'We have no idea if it is only our position that has been discovered. How do we know that your brother is not also aware of our scheme to capture humans and turn them into the undead here at Leroth? No, we have to act now while we can still have some small element of surprise. We have to change the way we go about spreading our zombie horde.' She looked down at her own body, lost in thought. Using her forefinger and thumb she plucked a large beetle from her abdomen, holding the thing in front of her face and examining it, before dropping it to the floor, where it scuttled back into the mass of insects that was her foot. 'Instead of harvesting humans here or anywhere else, we must use what we have already to maximum effect. We need to transport Leroth into an area full of humans, and let these two,' she nodded towards the zombies, 'wreak havoc.'

'Only two?'

'If we can put them among a big enough crowd, it should be enough.'

'And the Shield? What will its role be?'

'If I can maximize the Shield's operable distance, it will provide a wide arc of protection, stopping anything getting in or out.'

'How large can you make it?'

'The greater the distance, the weaker the barrier gets, so I will have to be careful not to stretch it too far. I would guess that a radius of a few hundred metres will be sustainable. It will also require all of my efforts and skill to keep it operational for any length of time.' She gave him a strange look. 'I will be vulnerable while I'm doing this, and will need you to look out for me.'

'It will have to be done at night. I shall be of no use to you if—'

'Not necessarily. The barrier will stop the sun's hurtful rays from destroying you. It will be like being under a glass dome.'

'But this Shield is not impenetrable? Could my brother gain access using sorcery?'

'Not easily. It would take a skilled practitioner of sorcery to even attempt such a thing.'

'There's the daughter – the dhampir.' The vampire frowned for a moment as he tried to recall the name of the half-human, half-vampire monstrosity that was his niece. 'Alexa. She has studied the dark arts.'

Helde waved this notion away. 'That child would not have the skill or power to attempt such a thing.'

She paused, then took a step towards him and continued in a low voice. 'We should strike at the heart of your brother's power base. We should show him what we are capable of, and that we are not cowed by this new ability of his!'

'London?'

'Why not? It will be the last thing he'd expect. Can you think of a suitable event that the humans might attend in great numbers?'

A terrible smile crept on to Caliban's face. His eyes narrowed. 'Yes, I think I know just the thing.'

8

Lucien closed his eyes behind his sunglasses and tipped his head back to let the sun bathe his face with its warmth and light. He was still unable to relax fully, his hands tightly gripping the balcony rail as he waited for the searing pain to begin, but it did not. It would not. The old witch was right.

After Hag had pulled her little stunt he had come out on to the balcony alone to reflect. Though he realized he should probably be careful this first time, after so many centuries, he was finding it hard to tear himself away and return indoors. He looked down at the back of his hand. His skin had changed colour even in this short period – not exactly a tan, but not the pale coloration he was used to seeing either. In truth, he was probably a little burned – but his skin would rejuvenate at vampire speed once he was inside. Reluctantly, he headed for the door to let it do just that.

'I can't go back there,' Trey said to Lucien.

They were sitting in the vampire's office, Lucien behind his desk and Trey in a chair opposite him, having come at the vampire's request. Despite having been warned by Tom about Lucien's experience in the sun earlier, Trey had not been prepared for the slight tan that the vampire sported on his face and hands. The teenager had never seen Lucien looking anything but deathly pale. He couldn't imagine what Alexa, his own daughter, would make of it. There was something else about the vampire too, Trey thought – an air of contentment almost. But the topic of conversation had soon put such lighter thoughts far from his mind.

'I understand the turmoil you must feel at the prospect of returning to Leroth, but—'

'No, Lucien, you don't understand.' Trey looked across at his guardian. 'Charles was killed in that place. I carried him out on my shoulders.'

Lucien met the teenager's look with his own, as if waiting for Trey to go on. When he didn't, Lucien aired what he thought was the real reason behind Trey's reluctance to revisit the place.

'You were almost killed in that place too.'

Trey shrugged. 'That's becoming a bit of an occupational hazard.'

'And in defending yourself,' the vampire went on as if he hadn't heard this last comment, 'you killed Gwendolin.' He raised a hand to stop his ward interrupting again. 'Let's not pretend the memory of *that* isn't bothering you every bit as much as what happened to your friend. I saw how you refused to meet Alexa's eyes when I revealed where my brother was.'

'Her mother's dead because of me.'

'No.' The vampire shook his head. 'The creature you

defended both yourself and Charles from was no longer Alexa's mother, any more than you are the boy I first met at the care home. You forget I once loved Gwendolin, and I can tell you that that woman ceased to exist a long, long time ago.' He sighed and raised an eyebrow at Trey. 'Alexa no more holds you responsible for her mother's death than I do. Besides, if you had not done what you did, I would not be here speaking to you today. Your stealing of Mynor's Globe from Leroth revived me.' He frowned, as if considering what he'd just said. He looked up at his young ward, a sad smile on his face. 'I wish there was some way that I could turn back the clock for you, Trey. To return you to a time when your world was not full of danger as it is now.'

Trey snorted. 'And how far would you turn the clock back?' He felt beneath his T-shirt for the amulet that hung there, remembering how Lucien had given it to him that first time they'd met, telling him to put it on and revealing that it had been his father's. It was this that enabled Trey to take on the upright, bipedal werewolf form he'd become accustomed to – a powerful, *thinking* creature rather than the terrifying four-legged nether-creature known as the Wolfen. He'd experienced what it was like to be in that particular werewolf form before when he'd Changed with the Pack in the Canadian forest, and he knew that as a Wolfen he could be a danger to the world and himself.

'It isn't as if my life changed the moment you walked into that care home, Lucien. Caliban had already murdered my parents and tried to have me killed when I was a baby, and he isn't going to stop until either he or I are dead. I'm lucky to have made it this far.' He shrugged in his guardian's direction. 'Besides, you saved me too, remember? If you hadn't come that day, I'd have been killed in the fire. I figure we're quits on that score.'

Trey realized that he hadn't had a chance to talk like this with his guardian for some time. It was strange, but Lucien always had a way of making Trey feel OK about whatever lay ahead, as if the teenager were able to draw from the vampire's own power and confidence. He smiled at the thought that his world was a less scary place with a vampire around, and the smile slipped from his face as Lucien's face was replaced by Caliban's in his mind.

'Tom tells me that you were considering leaving us.'

'That's not quite what I said.' Trey couldn't shake the mental image of Lucien's evil brother out of his head.

As if reading the young man's thoughts, his guardian nodded. 'You are more formidable than you think, and soon you will have a chance to unleash your powers and fulfil your destiny, Trey.'

There was a pause and Trey looked into Lucien's eyes, something that was never easy to do. 'You're talking about the legend again, aren't you?'

'I'm merely suggesting that *not* going to Leroth will do nothing to remove the threat against you. You can choose not to go, but sooner or later Caliban will catch up with you, maybe in Leroth and maybe not. Your destinies are linked, like the twisted strands of your own DNA, and you can either meet that destiny head-on or wait for it to find you.'

Trey considered this. 'I can run but I can't hide, is that it?'

'Something like that, yes.'

'That's what I thought.'

'I want you to know that I will not allow anything to happen to you, Trey. I will protect you like my own son. You must believe that.'

Trey studied the creature before him. He nodded his head. 'I do believe that, Lucien.'

The teenager stood up and turned to go, stopping at the door to face his guardian one more time. 'Thanks,' he said. A grin slowly crept on to his face. 'Oh, and by the way, the suntan thing,' he said, pointing. 'It suits you. Makes you look less . . . dead.'

'I shall bear that in mind.' Lucien looked down at the papers on his desk, but Trey caught the amused expression on his face as he did so.

He stepped out, closing the door behind him.

Now all he needed to do was straighten things out with Alexa.

9

The communication console next to the door beeped three times, and Alexa tapped the touch screen to answer it, noting that it was the front desk calling. She glanced across at the grill where the ham and cheese sandwich she was making for her breakfast was cooking.

'Hello?'

One of the guards on duty that morning spoke. 'Excuse me, Miss Charron, but there's a young lady in reception asking to see Mr Laporte. She says she's a friend of his.'

Alexa felt her insides clench. 'Let me guess,' she said. 'Blonde? Tall? Scarily blue eyes with a slight "desperate" look to them?'

There was a pause at the other end, and when the guard spoke again his embarrassment was evident in his voice. 'Er, well, she is blonde, yes. She says her name is Ella.'

Alexa was about to tell him that she had no idea if Trey was in, when she heard his bedroom door open and close, followed by the sound of his tuneless whistling as he crossed the living room in her direction. 'Tell her to wait downstairs, please. I'll let him know.' She tapped the screen again to sever the connection.

Trey walked in, the whistle dying on his lips when he saw her.

'Hi,' he said after a moment.

'Hi.'

There was an uncomfortable silence between them, neither of them knowing what to say next. It was Trey who finally spoke. 'Look, Lex. I've been meaning to talk to you since our last little . . . chat, and I really wanted to tell you that—'

'Your friend is downstairs,' she said, interrupting.

He gave her a puzzled look, and she sighed theatrically.

'Blondie? Your werewolf friend? The girl who saved your life? You know, the one you forgot to tell me about?'

'Don't be like that, please,' he said in a soft voice. 'I didn't invite her here. She just turned up—'

'Well, she's *just turned up* again. She's downstairs in the lobby, waiting for you.'

He frowned. 'I'm not expecting her.'

'It'd be rude to leave her down there waiting,' she said. 'You'd better go and see what she wants.'

He nodded, considering this. 'Why don't you come down with me? We could all go out somewhere together. You two could get to know each other a bit.'

Alexa raised an eyebrow at him and was about to say something when she sniffed the air. She looked behind her to see wisps of smoke coming from the grill. 'Shit!' she said, and hurried over to remove the blackened sandwich. 'I think I'll give your little idea a miss, thanks, Trey. I wouldn't want to be a gooseberry or anything like that, but be sure to give my regards to Blondie, won't you?'

'Ella,' Trey said in a tight voice. 'Her name is Ella.' He waited for Alexa to say something. By now, he was completely confused and frustrated by her hot and cold behaviour and he almost regretted coming in to try and patch things up between the two of them. Yesterday evening, after talking to Lucien, he'd gone down to the gym for a workout and used the time alone to think things through properly. He'd decided to be honest with her and tell her how he'd been struggling with things, but that even if she didn't feel the same way about him, he *did* have feelings for her.

Now all that had gone out of the window and it was as much as he could do to stop himself from telling her what a pain in the butt she was being.

Alexa swore again as she burned her finger on the grill pan. She glanced over her shoulder at him and tutted. 'Are you still here?'

'No,' he said. 'No, I'm not.' He turned and left the apartment, heading for the lobby.

'I wasn't expecting you,' Trey said to Ella as they left the building together.

'I thought I'd surprise you,' she said.

It was a bright, sunny day again, and Trey wished he'd brought his sunglasses with him as he squinted against the light.

There was a taxi waiting for them, and Ella headed

straight for it, holding the door open for him and beckoning for him to get inside.

'Where are we going?' he said as he climbed in.

'Like I said, it's a surprise.'

The taxi pulled away, the driver clearly knowing their destination even if Trey didn't. Ella sat close to him on the back seat, pointing out landmarks along the route, and asking him to tell her what they were. She laughed at his sketchy knowledge of the city he lived in, and when he shrugged and smiled back at her their eyes met, and her look became more serious. He could feel his face reddening, and she turned away to stare out of the window. They drove over Tower Bridge and were soon in an area of London that Trey had never visited before. The cab took a number of turns through a built-up residential area, navigating lefts and rights through mazy rat runs until it came out into a road ending in a scruffy-looking industrial estate. The place, and the houses that led up to it, had an abandoned and disused appearance. The cab headed for some old workshops on the estate, and Trey was about to suggest that the driver must have brought them to the wrong place when the vehicle pulled up outside what appeared to be a rundown car repairs garage. Ella took out her purse and paid the driver.

'Is this where you wanted to bring me?' Trey said, looking out at the derelict old building, the walls of which were made of corroded corrugated steel. It sat in a weed-strewn yard, and it was clear just from looking at it that the place had not been used for a number of years. The two main doors through which the cars must once have been driven were padlocked shut with a rusty chain and the windows were grimy with dust and dirt.

He gave Ella a puzzled look, but she only smiled enigmatically as she climbed out of the cab, which pulled away and left them. She headed for the small door to one side of the building, taking out a key from her bag and unlocking it. She nodded for him to go in ahead of her.

Trey walked into the place, which was surprisingly cool despite the hot sun outside. It was a small reception area – little more than a dilapidated old counter behind which a door led into the main body of the building. He half turned to look at Ella with a frown, but she nodded encouragingly for him to go round and through. He did so, pushing against the door which groaned in protest.

His eyes had already begun to adapt to the darkness inside the building, and as he stepped through he took in the large space. In the centre of the garage were two hydraulic platforms, both of which were raised up over the sunken bays beneath them. On one of these an old car still stood, the original paintwork obscured by the dust and grime that had accumulated on it over the years. Tools lay here and there, so that the general impression was of a place that had simply been abandoned by its former owners mid-use. But it was the strange array of manacles and chains on the floor between the two hydraulic platforms that caught Trey's eye. Two chains were secured to metal rings bolted into the ground. Trey thought it strange that, although the rings were clearly as old as the rest of the place, the chains threaded through them appeared to be brand new, the clean galvanized metal looking completely out of place against the forsaken, rusting equipment on display elsewhere in the workshop. He was about to comment on this when he noticed the small table to his left. Lying alone in the centre of the table was a hypodermic syringe filled with a clear liquid. Something about those chains and the syringe set every alarm bell ringing inside Trey, and he'd half turned to look at what Ella was doing behind him when he felt a sharp stabbing pain between his shoulders. He gasped, his hand flying back to seek out the source of the pain. He was too late.

Ella depressed the trigger of the Taser and watched as Trey flew forward on to the ground. The long wires leading to the barbed metal darts she'd fired into him snaked out from the front of the weapon, bouncing and twitching in response to the boy's convulsions as the electric current passed through him. She reached out with her other hand, calmly taking the syringe from the table. She'd practised this moment many times in her head, going over it again and again to ensure that she'd be able to react when it came to it. She released the trigger, stopping Trey's paroxysmal seizures long enough for her to step forward and jab the needle into his leg while depressing the plunger. The whole thing, from firing the Taser at him to injecting the drugs, was done in a matter of seconds.

Trey swore at her. He groaned and tried to get up, only

to be floored again when Ella momentarily depressed the trigger for a second time.

'Stay there and behave,' she said coldly. 'I'm assured by the man I bought them from that the drugs won't take long to work.' Then she added in a softer voice, 'Please, Trey, this is for your own good.'

'Let me ub, you bitsh,' Trey said, his lips and tongue not syncing with his brain. He tried to get to his knees again, but his vision swam, and he collapsed to the cold, hard floor.

Ella looked down at the figure. She puffed out her cheeks and nodded to herself, pleased with her work. She still had a number of things to do, but the hard part was over. Now it was just a matter of making Trey see sense.

10

Trey Laporte was trapped with the disembodied head of a demon floating in the air before him. Each and every time he tried to move – his arms and legs felt as if they were pinned to his sides – he sank deeper into the stuff all about him. The creature's face was a mass of ugly scars, which criss-crossed and overlapped each other in every direction as if they had been inflicted time and again over a long period – scars on top of scars on top of scars. One eye was milky and unseeing, but the other leered at the teenager as the creature opened its mouth and roared into the boy's face. As it did so, the demon transformed before Trey's eyes, morphing, twisting and compressing until it was Alexa's visage that loomed over him, her eyes rolling wildly with fear as she screamed over and over. Trey tried to call out to her, but found he could make no sound of his own in this place. Then, just as the nether-creature's face had melted away, so too did Alexa's, this time to be replaced with that of the vampire Caliban, who laughed at Trey's attempts to struggle free from whatever was holding him down. A huge throng of nether-creatures appeared behind the vampire, their bodies merging and coalescing into one great beast with hundreds of heads, which nodded and leered in unison as they stared down at him. Trey struggled again and felt himself sucked further down into the bubbling quicksand-like stuff all about him, his inevitable consumption by the mire eliciting a chorus of delighted shrieks from the crowd.

None of this is real.

Even in his terrified state, Trey was aware that he was hallucinating and that whatever Ella had injected into him was responsible for these terrible visions. On another level he knew that in reality he was chained and lying on the floor of the garage Ella had taken him to. But knowing that the nightmarish images weren't really there, and controlling the terror that resulted from them, were two different things.

He was up to his chin in the quicksand now, the ghastly smell that came from the stuff filling his head. 'You're not real!' he tried to shout, but again no sound came. He wanted to close his eyes, but this too proved impossible, and he was caught between the fear of the phantasmagoria before him and the even greater dread of slipping beneath the surface of the mire. The floating countenance of the vampire suddenly shot forward, lips peeled back over deadly fangs, ready to tear the boy's throat out. Instinctively, Trey threw himself backwards out of harm's way, the sudden movement submerging him for the last time beneath the sucking morass.

And then there was nothing but blackness, a complete lack of any light or sound. Trey willingly gave in to the dark, embracing the peace and calm that it provided, content to float in the womb-like void of unconsciousness.

*

When his eyes flickered open, the acrid stench of vomit filled Trey's nose and made his stomach clench in response. Even this tiny, involuntary movement elicited a low groan from the teenager whose head was pounding and whose tongue felt way too large for his mouth. He was lying on his side and could see the source of the stink on the floor in front of his face. He tried to get up but found that he could not. His legs were secured together at the ankles with some kind of manacles, and a band of metal, like a waist belt, was fastened around his abdomen, and it was to this that his wrists were handcuffed. Bound in this way, he was forced to shuffle on his side away from the pool of filth, every movement resulting in a knifing pain in his head that caused him to groan and whimper. Trey wished he were back in that black void. He wanted nothing more than to curl up into a small, tight ball and allow the darkness to return, but he resisted the urge, taking a deep breath and tipping his head backwards instead, straining to see what he could. The workshop was dark, but Trey thought he could sense somebody in the shadows watching him. He shifted his weight, throwing his hips up and over – the terrible, harsh racket of the chains crashing into each other and the floor filled the place for a moment – so he was lying face down. The concrete floor beneath him was black with car oil that had been spilt over it through the years, and the smell of it filled his nostrils. At least it was better than the puke. He bucked his body and somehow succeeded in getting his knees beneath him. The metal girdle about his waist had two chains snaking out from either side of it, and these were fixed on short chains to the hoops in the floor he'd seen when he first entered this place. The set-up meant there was no way that he could get fully to his feet, and he was forced to kneel with his arms by his sides.

'I'd try and stay still for a while yet if I were you,' Ella said, stepping out of the gloom and approaching him. 'I might have got the dosage of that sedative a bit wrong.' She was swapping something between her hands, pouring it from one to the other like grains of sand. Except it wasn't sand. The dull silver colour of the chain caught Trey's eye, and he knew without needing to look down towards his own chest that she'd removed the amulet he wore round his neck.

Ella followed the direction of his gaze and smiled. 'I didn't want you just morphing into that wolf-man creature you become with this thing on and undoing all of my efforts to get you here.'

'What's going on?' Trey said, swallowing hard to try and moisten his dry and sore throat. 'Why have you brought me here like this?'

'Would you like some water?'

Trey glared back at her.

'It's for your own safety, Trey. You'll thank me for this one day.'

Trey lowered his head and studied the floor between his knees, trying to make some sense of what she was saying.

'I don't know what's up with you, Ella, but you'd better unlock me from these chains and let me out of here. You have no idea what is going on in this world right now, because if you did, you'd know that I can't be here. I need to get back to Lucien and—'

'And what, Trey? Hmm? What is so important about your vampire friend that you're willing to sacrifice your life for him? The fight between him and his lunatic brother is not your fight, Trey. Let the vampires tear each other apart. Let Caliban take over the human realm and subjugate everyone on it. What does that have to do with you and me and our kind?' She looked down at him, shaking her head. 'You're *not* human. You're a lycanthrope just like me. And whatever they've told you about your duty or your . . . destiny, well, it's all lies!'

Trey struggled to take in everything he was hearing. The waves of pain and nausea made it difficult for him to concentrate, and he frowned as he tried to put together what he'd just heard. Ella knew about the forthcoming attack by Caliban. It occurred to him that she might be working for the vampire, but he quickly dismissed the idea. He would already be dead if that were the case. No, she must have found out about it from another source – perhaps she had a contact inside Lucien's organization, somebody she'd befriended so that she could find things out about Trey. He shook his head, realizing that it didn't matter how she'd found out. What *did* matter was that she'd captured him to stop him taking any role in defending against it. But why?

'What am I doing here?'

'You're my . . . guest, albeit a reluctant one at the moment, but that will change, Trey, you'll see. We have your best interests at heart?'

'We?'

'Marcus and me.'

'Marcus?'

'He's joining us soon. In fact, he should be boarding a plane in the next few days. I called him and told him to come.'

'Does he know that you've kidnapped me?'

'That's a rather emotive expression.' She snorted and shook her head. 'Kidnap indeed!'

'He doesn't, does he? If he did, he'd be here right now.'

'Like I said, I have your very best interests at heart.'

'Really?' Trey let out a short derisive laugh. 'Is that why I'm in chains? Is that why you injected me with goodness knows what drugs? Forgive me, Ella, but I think I preferred it when I didn't have you looking out for me!'

'You're wrong. You need us as much as we need you. You just don't know it yet. And when I say *we*, I mean lycanthropes – your own kind. We need you with us, not gallivanting around with some bloodsucking freak trying to save the world.' She took a deep breath. 'Let the vamps war against each other. And when they're done, we'll emerge as the strongest force that this world has ever seen.'

Trey looked up at her then, his face a mask of incredulity. This was not the Ella he'd met and befriended in Canada.

And this certainly was not the girl who'd saved his life. She was like a different person, as if possessed by some evil spirit who spoke and acted through her, and for a moment Trey wondered if this were the case, if some denizen of the Netherworld were controlling her, because there was no way that the caring, giving person he had left not that long ago in Canada could be this thing before him now.

She nodded as though reading his thoughts. 'You don't like the new me, do you? Well, that's too bad because the meek and pathetic Ella you once knew has gone . . . forever.'

'What's happened to you?'

'I woke up.' She snorted and twisted her face into a sneer. 'That's right, I woke up to the reality of what I really was. After you left Canada I went back to Norway to try and start my life again. But I didn't know what it was like to be without the Pack, Trey. I had no idea how much I would miss it – miss the power and the . . . the sense of belonging. And then I had a full-moon Change. You know, one of those "turn-into-a-savage-murderous-beast-and-not-remember-anything-about-it" Changes?' She shook her head. 'I was too late getting to my lock-down. I changed before I could make myself secure.' When she looked at Trey again, there was a terrible expression on her face. 'You know I told you that my parents didn't want anything to do with me?'

Trey nodded.

'They're dead. They died that night.'

A long and terrible silence hung between them as Trey took this in.

'I'm sorry,' he said in a low voice.

'I need the Pack, Trey.' Ella's voice matched Trey's and he had to strain to hear her. 'I was the female Alpha, for heaven's sake. I was at the centre of that beautiful living thing of power, and I can't just give it up.'

'You don't need me though. It only takes three lycos to get together to make the controlled Change without the moon possible. There's you, and Marcus and Lawrence. Lawrence loved the Pack. I'm sure he'd—'

'Lawrence is dead.'

'Dead?' Trey thought about the gangly ginger-headed youth he'd met during his time in Canada with the Wolfen pack members. It wasn't possible he could be dead.

'It seems Marcus and I are not alone in needing the Pack. When we disbanded following Jurgen's death, we all went our separate ways. But the bond we'd formed between us was too strong. Lawrence left a note saying he couldn't go on any longer, and that he'd rather be dead than suffer a life alone. They found his body floating in a river.' During this explanation Ella had stared out into nothingness, lost in her own memories, but now her eyes snapped back to her captive. 'No. You have to become our third member, Trey. You're all we have left.'

'You've lost your mind.'

She paused, as if considering this. 'You've never felt it, have you? Never felt the keening wrench of separation. And do you know why? Because of this.' She hoisted the silver amulet in her hand, letting the chain play out between her fingers until it hung down, swinging gently to and fro. 'This makes you into the lone wolf that you've become, Trey. It keeps you away from your own kind. It keeps you bound to the likes of Lucien Charron.' She looked down at the thing and shook her head, before adding, 'At least it did.' She gathered up the chain in her hand again and placed it in her pocket before turning to walk away.

'Wait, Ella, please. You have no idea what you're doing. My friends! They're in terrible danger. We all are!'

'I'll bring you some food and water,' she called over her shoulder as she disappeared through the door leading out of the workshop. 'And then you and I need to have a little chat about your *friends*.'

11

Tom was emerging from the armoury on the first floor when he saw Lucien walking through the office. It was unusual to see the vampire up and about so early in the morning, and there was something about the look on his friend's face that told Tom something was seriously wrong.

'Mrs Magilton has just informed me that Trey did not sleep in his bed last night.' Lucien said.

Tom reached for the mobile phone in his pocket.

'I've tried that. His phone is dead.'

The two friends shared a look, neither wishing to voice the thoughts they were both having at that moment. Both were reminded of their recent conversations with the teenager, and how he'd hinted at a desire to run away from everything. Tom was the first to break away, giving Lucien one brief nod before striding off in the direction of his office, already barking instructions into the communications earpiece he wore. Before he entered, he turned and called across to his boss, 'Find Hag and Alexa, especially Alexa. One of them may have an idea where he is.'

The three of them, Lucien, Tom and Alexa, sat around the large table in the kitchen eyeing each other nervously. Hag had already told Lucien that she would not be joining them, pointing out that she had no idea where the boy was, and that her time would be better spent by trying to locate him using sorcery.

'We have to face the fact that Trey might have simply gone of his own accord, and that he's decided that he no longer wants any part of this,' Lucien said with a vague gesture of his hand.

'I don't buy that,' Tom said.

'You yourself told me that he'd been very down lately, and that he'd suggested to you that he'd considered simply walking away. Why is it so hard to believe?'

'Because the boy was just voicing his fears about whatever lies ahead. He'd no more walk out on us than you or I would.'

'You don't know that for certain, Tom.'

'Yes I do. And so do you, Lucien.' Tom let out a long sigh and eyed his boss. 'Are you honestly going to sit there and tell me you think that boy could just up and leave like that, without so much as a goodbye?'

The vampire shook his head. 'Everything I know about Trey tells me that you're right. But we don't know what's going on inside his head, do we? And we can't begin to guess how psychologically damaged he was after his experiences in the Netherworld.' He paused and added in a lower voice, 'Everybody and everything has a breaking point, Tom. Even you . . . or me.'

The Irishman turned to look at Alexa, who'd been

silent throughout all this, staring at the table and chewing nervously at the inside of her mouth.

'Tell us about this girl again.'

'She turned up downstairs yesterday. Trey wasn't expecting her, but he went down to see her.'

'And just left with her? Without telling anyone that he was going?'

'I've told you, it's all my fault,' Alexa said in a low voice. 'We had a row. Another one. I've been a complete bitch to Trey over the last couple of days, and he's probably gone off with this girl because of that.'

'Security says that they left together in a taxi,' Tom said. 'We've looked at the CCTV images from the front of the building, and we found the cab's registration number, but so far we haven't managed to track down the driver. I've put some good people on it, so it's only a matter of time.'

Lucien looked across at his daughter. 'This girl is a lycanthrope and a member of the LG78, you say?'

'Yes, but she's not a threat to Trey. She saved his life, for heaven's sake!'

Lucien pursed his lips, frown lines etching his forehead as he took this in.

'Maybe Trey *has* just decided to stay out for the night. Maybe he stayed at this girl's place.' He glanced across at his daughter. 'I'm sorry,' he added.

'No!' Tom said, banging his hand on the table. 'The Trey Laporte I know and care about is not some thoughtless

86

Lothario who'd just go off to a girl's house for the night. It doesn't make any sense. *Trey's not like that!'*

Lucien held up his hand. 'Nevertheless, we can't assume that our young ward's disappearance is as a result of foul play. He left of his own free will, and went off with a trusted friend. Let's get the number of this cab and see where that avenue of investigation takes us. In the meantime, I'll talk to Hag to see how she's getting on with her efforts to find him.'

'I'm going to put more of our people on it. I'm—'

'No,' Lucien interrupted. 'I will not have any more personnel diverted from our main objective of discovering where and how Caliban plans to stage his attack. That has to remain our primary focus. He could move Leroth at any moment. As soon as he does we will need to react.'

The vampire and the Irishman stared hard at each other for a long time, and Alexa looked between the two of them uncomfortably.

'You're the boss,' Tom said eventually through gritted teeth.

The vampire looked as if he was about to respond, but instead he stood, turned on his heel and left the room.

Tom watched his friend leave. He looked down at his hands, which were clenched into two tight fists on the table surface.

'My father's just worried, Tom. Worried and frightened like the rest of us. He cares about Trey as much as you do – you know that.'

Alexa placed her hand over one of the Irishman's fists, and gave it a little shake. There was nothing else to say. She got up and left, her head already filled with ideas about how she might go about locating Trey.

12

Caliban watched the sorceress as she prepared herself to perform the magic necessary to transport the tower and then create the impenetrable barrier around it. She had invited him down here, into the bowels of this place, to see her discovery for himself, walking him through a maze of tunnels carved into the black rock until they'd arrived at the entrance to the small chamber. Upstairs, waiting at ground level in the place from which she would release them, were the zombies. The sorceress entered the small space almost reverentially, turning and beckoning for the vampire to join her. She pointed at the far wall, a number of smaller insects dropping from her arm as she did so.

'There it is,' she said in a low, reverential tone.

The vampire struggled to hide his disappointment. He wasn't sure what he'd been expecting, but this rough, blank stone wall certainly was not it.

'That's the source of the Shield?' he'd asked.

'Yes! Can't you feel the power coming from it?'

The vampire shook his head, frown lines furrowing his brow.

'No, I must admit I can't. But then again, I'm not as

attuned to these things as you are.' He gave her a look that was half smile, half sneer.

'You'll stay?' she asked. 'You'll stay and witness me perform the ritual? It has not been carried out for millennia, and it will require all of my considerable power and skills.'

Caliban looked at the sorceress. Unlike some of his kind, he had little interest in dark magic. For him it was merely a means to an end, a necessary evil. He would have refused, therefore, had he not sensed that the creature by his side wanted him to observe the feat she was about to perform.

'Of course,' he said with a nod of his head. 'It will be an honour to watch you at work, Helde.'

She'd returned the gesture and then started the mental preparations necessary to carry out the sorcery.

That had been fifteen minutes ago, and now the vampire was beginning to lose patience as he watched her pacing to and fro, muttering under her breath one moment, her voice rising to a maniacal babble the next. He was about to ask her what was taking so long when she abruptly turned on her heel and approached the wall. Reaching up, she placed her hands, fingers splayed wide, on the rock surface.

'Uzshnek beil gorlok,' she said in a high, loud voice.

The rock beneath her insect hands began to glow, the light spreading out quickly like two pools of liquid eager to merge and unite. Within seconds the entire wall was ablaze with a dazzling light that made the vampire screw up his eyes and turn his head away.

'What is that?' he said.

'The Shield!' she shouted back. 'It is the Shield.'

She lowered her head again, and intoned more ancient words. Caliban felt a harsh tugging sensation inside him, and knew that this was a result of the sorceress translocating the tower from Iceland to the new location he'd given her in London. The blinding light still filled the room, and it was as much as the vampire could do to look through the tiniest of eye-slits at the sorceress. More wailing, more shouts and screams.

It was almost too much for him to bear. He was about to leave when there was an impossibly deep, penetrating *THUMP!* and a shockwave of immense power and energy flew out in all directions, causing him to gasp as it passed through his body. The light from the wall faded and was gone.

Helde slumped forward against the stone, the black-bodied creatures dropping from her in a torrent, and she would have fallen had Caliban not rushed to her side to support her as best he could. She leaned against him, raising her head and managing to give him a brief smile.

'It is done,' she whispered and closed her eyes.

He looked at the thing in his arms. She seemed utterly spent, and he remembered what she'd said about how difficult it would be for her to maintain the Shield for any length of time. 'How long can you keep it in place?'

'I'm not sure,' she said. 'I will regain some strength soon enough, but we should hurry to release the two undead creatures.'

'Yes,' he said. 'I will carry you upstairs . . . to my rooms at the top of the tower.'

'Thank you.'

The vampire nodded down at her. She seemed to have fainted away. He took her in his arms and left the room.

13

Hag sat in the chair opposite Lucien and Tom, her eyes closed, and while she made no sound, her lips moved as she silently mouthed words in an ancient tongue. She paused, frowned and tilted her head a little to one side, as if trying hard to listen for someone or something. Tom couldn't take his eyes away from the ballpoint pen which had risen into the air as a result of the magic she was conjuring when the sorceress had started her spell. The thing hovered just in front of her, quivering violently as if it might fly off in any direction at a moment's notice. In addition to the pen, Hag's thin grey hair, which normally hung in a straggled mess around her face, stood up all over, giving her a comical, cartoon-like appearance.

'He's alive,' she said in a low voice. 'The boy's alive, but he's . . . sick. No, not sick . . . something else.'

'Something else?' Tom said. 'What's that supposed to mean, for heaven's sake?'

The old woman's already wrinkled brow furrowed even more.

'It's strange, but everything is mixed up. Maybe it's drugs.'

'No way!' Tom said, shaking his head. 'Trey's not the sort of kid to take drugs. You must be—'

'Quiet, you fool!' the old woman hissed. 'How am I supposed to concentrate with you jibber-jabbering all the time?'

Tom somehow managed to hold his tongue, but his face was pinched and set as he fought the anger the sorceress always seemed to ignite within him. He lifted one hand and gesticulated at the old woman with two fingers.

'I might have my eyes shut, but I know what you're doing, you foolish oaf. If you do that again I shall have to think of some way to teach you respect for your elders; maybe you'd like to try not *having* fingers for a few days? I can do that, you know.'

'Stop it, the pair of you,' Lucien commanded in a low voice. 'Hag, what more can you tell us? Where is Trey?'

The old woman shook her head, her eyes still firmly closed. 'I can't make it out. The signals I'm getting are confused and chaotic.'

Tom was on his feet now. 'This is pointless,' he said.

Lucien leaned forward in his chair. When he spoke his voice was low and controlled, but there was no mistaking the urgency in it. 'Is there some way you can deduce if he's Changed at any point since he disappeared?'

'Since he was *taken*,' Tom said, correcting the vampire. 'That boy's in trouble – I can sense it.'

Lucien shot a withering look at his friend.

The sorceress shook her head. 'I don't believe he has transformed since we last saw him, no.'

Lucien nodded at Tom. 'So wherever he is, he doesn't

feel in any danger. Otherwise he would have Changed in order to defend himself.'

'That's assuming he was able to. Hag just said that he's been drugged.'

Lucien rubbed at his eyes with the finger and thumb of one hand, thinking everything through again. 'Hag, what can you tell me about Trey's—'

The old woman let out a sudden harsh cry, her body jerking violently as if some galvanizing current had been passed through it. She sat bolt upright and opened her eyes wide, staring straight ahead into those of the vampire.

'He's here!'

'Trey? But I thought you just said—'

The old woman gave an angry hiss and shook her head. 'Your *brother*, Caliban. He's here.'

Tom smashed his fist on to the tabletop. 'I told you he had the boy! Where is he?'

Hag looked up at the Irishman and shook her head. 'He does not have the lycanthrope.'

She was visibly shaken. 'The vampire lord has just arrived in this city. He and that abomination, Helde, have brought Leroth right here. I felt it.'

There was a loud knock on the door. One of the demons in Lucien's employ opened it and stepped in, not waiting for an invitation. The expression on the nether-creature's face matched that on the sorceress's. 'We've had reports of a massive disruption in—'

'We know,' Lucien said, interrupting. 'It's Caliban.

He has relocated Leroth. Do we have an exact fix on his position?'

'We're double-checking, but we're fairly certain that we've triangulated the signals to a point in West London. On the Fulham Road.'

Lucien frowned.

'Right opposite the football stadium. One of the humans in the office says that it's a match day today. The place will be teeming with people going to the game.'

Lucien gave Tom a terrible look as the full meaning of what he'd just been told began to dawn on him.

'He's going to release zombies into that crowd.' He shook his head in disbelief. 'It'll be a massacre.'

'We have to get there and stop him. Right now,' Tom said, already moving to the door.

'That's not going to be as easy as you might think,' Hag said in a strange voice. 'Helde has activated the Shield.'

Alexa went straight to the office as soon as she heard the alarm, arriving to find the place swarming with humans and nether-creatures, a chaos of movement and noise as each of them busily went about their tasks, a TV in the background blaring the breaking news. Tom was bawling orders to people across the room one moment and yelling into his communications headset the next.

She scanned the room. Her father was an oasis of calm. He'd assembled a number of nether-creatures, and was talking to them each in turn, no doubt explaining their roles in the forthcoming conflict.

Just the manic sound of the place was enough to set her nerves on edge, and she fought to repress the fear which rose in her every time she dared to consider what might lie ahead in the next few hours.

She walked over to her father.

'. . . beheading is the best method. If that fails, dismemberment of the legs will serve as a temporary solution, but you must remember to go back and finish the job. The zombie will still be alive and a potential danger to any human who steps too near to it.' The demons around him nodded their heads. 'Remember, when you enter the cordon provided by this Shield, you are effectively in a place which is neither in the human realm nor in the Netherworld. It's a kind of limbo between the two. As such, the human disguises that you use to hide yourselves here will be compromised, and any humans will be able to see beyond that facade to what you really are, and they're going to be as terrified of *you* as they are of the zombies. Please bear that in mind. We can no longer pretend to the human world that the Netherworld does not exist, but we don't want people running away from us, only to plough straight into a group of undead flesh-eaters, do we? It'll be chaotic in there, but you must always bear in mind that our primary goal is to save lives and remove the threat. The more people we can stop being *turned,* the less carnage we will leave behind us when this is finished. Remember, even the zombies were innocent human beings not so long ago.'

He looked up and saw Alexa standing there. 'That'll be all for now. We'll meet at the armoury in twenty minutes. As soon as Tom has equipped us all we'll be setting off.'

He left the demons to talk among themselves, and moved over to Alexa. Without a word, he gently took her by the elbow and steered her towards one of the meeting rooms. Once inside, he closed the door behind him, shielding them both from the worst of the din.

'So it's happened,' Alexa said. 'Caliban has made his final bid to take over the human world. Nothing will ever be the same again, will it?'

Lucien shook his head gravely.

'And you're leaving in the next twenty minutes?'

'I notice that you didn't say "we're leaving".'

'No.'

A silence stretched out between them.

'Look, I know you could use my sorcery skills,' Alexa continued, 'but Hag is more skilful and powerful than I'll ever be.'

'That may or may not be true. But you're right, Hag should be capable of getting us inside the Shield. Hopefully.'

'I'm going to try and find Trey.'

Her father looked at her, the merest touch of a smile forming on his lips before disappearing again. 'I hoped you would.'

'But—'

'That is why I have asked Hag to spend some time with

you before we leave to make a few suggestions. She has a theory about how you might be able to locate him, even though she herself has failed.' He paused for a moment, studying the floor and frowning. 'I think I have allowed my own fear about what lies ahead to cloud my judgement concerning Trey. I should have realized that he would never have left us simply because he was afraid. He would certainly never have left *you* like that.'

'Did . . . did I just hear right? Did you say that *you* were frightened?'

He smiled at her fully then, his lips peeling back to show off his fangs to full effect. 'Yes, Alexa. Even an ancient creature like your father can still feel fear every now and again.' When he next spoke he was all business. 'I'm allocating two of our people to go with you when you set off to find Trey. If and when you do, you're both to come back here and await instructions from me. You're not to come down to Leroth, do you understand that? You must both ignore everything that I've said about Trey and Caliban and destiny. Trey is not ready to face my brother yet. Just get him back here and keep each other safe. Is that clear?'

'I'll find him,' Alexa said.

'Thank you.'

They stood then, just looking at each other, neither of them wanting to air their thoughts or anxieties.

'Please be careful,' her father said eventually.

'I will,' she nodded.

Lucien stepped forward and pulled his daughter into his

arms. 'You mean more to me than you could ever possibly know.'

Alexa returned the embrace, wrapping her arms round her father and breathing in the smell of his cologne. She hugged him tight, hoping against hope that this was not the last time she would do so.

14

Trey lay on the floor motionless, and would have appeared dead to anyone looking down on him if it were not for the facial tics and frowns that altered his expression every now and then.

Ella stared at the figure sprawled out on the cold surface. She'd been forced to inject him again, and she guessed he was hallucinating behind those closed eyelids. She was glad she'd covered him with a blanket. It kept him warm, but it also meant she didn't have to look at the manacles and chains she'd had to use to keep him here.

It's for his own good, she told herself again.

She considered what had just happened.

She'd told him a lie. A lie she thought would help to free him from what he saw as his obligations to the vampire and his cohorts. On reflection it wasn't the smartest thing to do, but he'd refused to listen to her when she explained again how he didn't belong with them. That *they* were the thing stopping him seeing reason.

So she'd told him that both Lucien and his dhampir daughter were dead, killed in a fight with the vampire's brother. She'd been taken aback by the reaction. He'd flown into an apoplectic rage the like of which she'd never seen before, throwing himself against his restraints, screaming and wailing at her until she thought he would damage himself or, worse, enforce a Change as she'd seen other lycanthropes do when they became so worked up. She had to admit that the entire episode had shaken her up. She had no idea of the depth of feeling he had for those people. How could she? He'd come to Canada to get away from them, hadn't he? To find his uncle and start a new life. She'd thought he might damage himself, so she'd quickly tasered him and injected him again.

She hadn't expected this much trouble from him. She'd thought that once she'd explained to him the error of his ways he'd understand she was right – that as a werewolf, he belonged with her and others like her. That he was the perfect Alpha male partner for her.

She guessed he would be different when he woke up this time. His reaction had been to the shock of the news. He'd soon see that she was right.

She put her hand in her pocket and fingered the links of the silver chain she'd removed from his neck. Pulling her hand out, she looked down at the jumble of tiny metal hoops with the small silver fist amulet that gave Trey so much control over his lycanthrope powers. She'd felt the magic that existed in the thing when she'd momentarily held it in the woods in Canada, and Trey's Uncle Frank had told her it was a precious object to her kind: an amulet rumoured to have been created by Theiss – an ancient werewolf charged with protecting humankind from the creatures of the Netherworld. He had been burned at the stake, but his talisman had survived and been passed down the centuries to those of his bloodline.

If she'd had such a thing when she'd returned home from Canada, maybe her parents would not—

She hissed at herself, shaking her head to dislodge the unbidden memory.

No, she would destroy the amulet. That too was a bond to the vampire, Lucien, designed to keep Trey under his influence and control. Why else would the vampire have given it to him? She would break that bond by dismantling it. Later. She curled her fingers round the chain and returned it to her pocket.

The hallucinations were as terrifying this time as they had been before – nightmarish scenes of evil, filled with nether-creatures all out to destroy him and those he cared about. They were everywhere – hissing, snarling, roaring and gibbering at him. He saw his dead friends among them, especially Alexa. A glimpse of her through a gap in the hideous faces, looking back at him beseechingly. He would charge in her direction, only to be pushed back by the laughing, mocking horde. Then the gap would close and she'd be gone. Trey opened his mouth and tried to scream, and as he did so there was an abrupt silence; the demonic creatures that made up the nightmare host looked around in alarm, trying to find the source of power they could suddenly sense all about them.

Trey felt it too, but whereas the nether-creatures were filled with fear at this new authority, Trey felt a calmness and relief. He too looked about him for what it might be.

It was a man. An old man with a beard, dressed in a robe. Even in his delirium, Trey could not help but wish his subconscious had come up with something less . . . biblical. The old man strode through the throngs of demons and djinn, and as he did so the flames that covered his body from head to toe set them on fire, causing them to screech and wail in agony. The flames spread, jumping from creature to creature until the horde was consumed by them and eventually disappeared from sight.

The man stood before Trey, his eyes narrowed as he considered the boy. He seemed not to notice the conflagration that consumed him, and Trey could feel no heat from the blaze, despite the ferocity with which it burned.

'Theiss,' Trey said, knowing without a doubt who it was.

'You must break free, young lycanthrope,' the figure said. 'You must escape this place. The final fight is coming, and you must be there.'

'I can't. I'm chained up. I'm somewhere on a garage floor, pumped full of drugs that are making me hallucinate things like *you*!'

'You will not escape?'

'I CAN'T!'

The old man studied him, his brows still beetled as he stared at the youngster.

'You are of my blood, Trey Laporte. You are of a long line of lycanthropes who were charged with defending the earth against those who would enslave it. Do not tell me that you cannot escape.'

'She's taken the amulet!' Trey said. Part of him wondered why he was continuing this conversation with this spectre of his mind. 'For all I know, she's thrown it off a bridge into the river.'

The old man contemplated this before continuing. 'Do you still think that a son of Theiss needs such a thing? That a true-blood lycanthrope who is directly descended from the thing's creator has any need of such a . . . trinket?'

Trey realized that although they seemed to be talking – his mouth shaping the words and moving in the normal way – no sound actually came from either of them in this place.

'If I don't wear the amulet I can't Change at will on my own. And even if I could, it would not be into the type of werewolf I have been up until now! I'd become a . . . terrible thing. I'd have no control over my urges. I'd become a killer!'

'And how do you know this? How do you know what you would become and what you would do?'

'What does it matter anyway? They're dead! Alexa's dead and neither you nor I nor that amulet is ever going to bring her back. I wasn't there to help her! I wasn't there to stop Caliban.'

'You are of my blood, Trey Laporte. You are—'

Trey shook his head. 'I'm not listening to you! You're

not real. NONE OF THIS IS REAL! IT'S ALL JUST ANOTHER TRICK!'

'You don't have to listen to me, lycanthrope. You need to listen to yourself.'

Trey watched as the old man's face changed, his features becoming smoother and less wrinkled. His long chin became squarer and stronger and his eyes, as they changed from grey to brown, took on an altogether different look. The flames still consumed the face, but Trey recognized his father immediately.

Daniel Laporte never spoke. He looked down at his son, his eyes full of sadness as if he were sharing the pain that his child was going through. But there was something else in the look he gave Trey: there was hope. As if sensing the boy had picked up on this, he smiled and nodded. But even the appearance of his father could not lift Trey out of the despair he felt, and as he watched, his father began to fade. Trey tried to move only to find he was cemented in place. He called out to his dad, but to no avail. Daniel Laporte disappeared and was replaced by a darkness that fell upon Trey and carried him away with it. Just before it did, the thought occurred to him that this blackness was not unlike death. He might even be dead. And he realized that he didn't care any longer.

15

With forty minutes to go until the start of the match, the streets around Stamford Bridge football ground were packed with the supporters of both sides, all clad in their team's colours, jostling and pressing up against each other as they made their way towards the stadium under the watchful eye of the police. The air was thick with the smells of fast food coming from the numerous mobile cabins lining the way, and the bright sunshine ensured that a festival-like atmosphere was beginning to develop, despite the fierce rivalry between the two teams' supporters. It was a London derby: Chelsea, the home side, were taking on north London opposition Arsenal, and the match was a sell-out. A high police presence was everywhere, and as the fans got nearer to the stadium they were segregated by the uniformed officers and funnelled into the ground separately to avoid the possibility of any trouble.

Loud and raucous songs rang out from various factions as they caught sight of a rival element, and these were answered with chants from the opposition, decrying the other team and its players. A general feeling of suppressed menace was in the air, but there was no sign that this might spill over into violence.

107

Robert Holt and his young son, Jake, were waiting in the queue at a burger van. The father kept a hand on the boy's shoulder to ensure that the youngster couldn't get separated from him. The crowds were bigger than they'd experienced during their previous two trips to the football, but Jake had recently fallen in love with the game, and Robert promised he'd get them tickets for the weekend of the boy's birthday.

Robert had just put his order in for their cheeseburgers when he heard a loud roaring sound away to his right. He winced with the pain the noise created inside his ears, and he glanced down to see that Jake had clamped his hands against the side of his head to muffle the worst of the racket.

It was like the sound of a huge jet engine – a wall of noise that shook everything around it. He glanced about him and saw that other people were equally disturbed by the din, their faces screwed up in discomfort as they sought the source of the noise. Robert pulled his son towards him, bending forwards so that he could nod at the boy, silently asking if he was OK.

'IT'S VERY LOUD!' Jake shouted back at his father. 'WHAT IS IT?'

Robert gave a shrug and shook his head. He frowned, watching as his son's facial expression turned from one of discomfort to a wide-eyed look of fear and disbelief at whatever he'd seen over his dad's shoulder. Robert turned to see what it was the boy had witnessed. That was when he saw the source of the tumult for the first time. There, in the middle of the Fulham Road, was a black tower that had no place in this world. It had materialized out of nowhere, the inky dark rocks that made up the base of the thing replacing the painted brickwork of the houses and shops that had once stood there. Where those buildings, or the people might have been inside them, had gone was unclear. He let his eyes travel up the ghastly citadel, his panic rising as he did so. It was a vision which would haunt Robert Holt's dreams for evermore.

Now everyone in the street had turned to face the monolith, a look of utter incredulity on each and every face as they took in its gothic grandeur. It towered up into the heavens, a black stiletto blade that dwarfed the other buildings around it and resonated with a dark force that struck terror into those that looked upon it.

Robert Holt could feel the fear pouring off his son; it matched his own. He hugged the boy to him, murmuring comforting words, knowing that he could not let his son sense the horror, bafflement and despair he truly felt. Because Robert was sure of one thing: whatever that dark tower was, it spelled danger for everyone who had seen it.

Father and son both flinched as a loud boom came from the tower. Looking up again, they saw a wave radiating from the structure, the air shimmering and appearing to *bend* as the invisible force spread ever outward. Screams and shouts of panic could be heard from all sides, and people began to run in every direction, hoping to escape the malevolent force.

Robert grabbed his son's hand and tried to pull him around the back of the burger van, but the boy was frozen to the spot. When the wave passed through them they cried out in unison. They had been touched by evil, of that they were certain, and the wrenching of their insides as the wave penetrated them was nothing compared to the feeling of doom they were left with on its passing.

There was a moment of stillness then. A perfect stop. Until suddenly the sky turned a dark and terrible purple, the air itself taking on a strange aspect, so that looking through it was like peering through the bottom of a glass bottle. At the same time, the air was filled with a putrid stench of something rotten and foul and fetid that made everyone gag and cover their mouths and noses with their hands.

The Shield had been activated. It produced an impenetrable dome-like perimeter around the central point of the tower, extending the estate of Leroth by 500 metres in all directions and bringing the Netherworld to the area confined within it. Everything and everyone inside was trapped. There was no way in or out. There was no communication with the outside world. There was no hope of escape.

16

Alexa sat alone in the living room. The apartment hadn't been this quiet in weeks, and the silence was more than a little unnerving. She shifted her weight, the soft white leather beneath her sighing in response.

She began to prepare herself for what lay ahead, going through the mental processes that Hag had described to her before she had left with her father and the others. Performing any kind of sorcery was never easy, but trying to combine two separate and very different spells was going to require all her effort and skills.

Although under a great deal of stress and pressure herself, Hag had found the time to take the teenager into one of the meeting rooms and explain her theory on how Alexa could locate the whereabouts of Trey.

'You must try to amalgamate the locating spell I used earlier in front of your father and Tom with the thought transfer spell that you are already very adept at. I believe that the special bond you share with the young lycanthrope will allow you to communicate with him in this manner. Sadly, I could not, and the signals that I was picking up were jumbled and chaotic.'

'But it's not possible to use the thought transfer spell

over any great distance – a few hundred metres is about the most I've ever managed.'

'That's why you're merging that spell with the location one – piggybacking one on the other, if you like.' The old woman paused and thought for a moment. 'It will be difficult, *very* difficult, but I believe you can do it.' She looked at the girl and nodded encouragingly. 'You are more powerful than I was at your age, Alexa, and you're going to be a great sorceress one day.'

'Thank you, but—'

'You'll need to be careful about the side effects of the sorcery. The thought transfer spell creates thermal energy as a by-product and the location magic generates kinetic energy. What the result of combining them will be is anyone's guess.'

Tom and Lucien appeared in the doorway.

Alexa looked up at her father and managed a brave smile.

'All set to go?' Hag asked.

'Yes, we're ready.' Lucien looked at his daughter. 'Have the two of you discussed the best way to find Trey?'

'Yes,' the old woman said, getting to her feet and shuffling towards the two men. 'She'll be fine. We should go. Now. Let's not all stand around getting mushy – it'll serve none of us any good.' She laid a hand on Alexa's arm as she passed, and in a low voice meant only for the girl's ears added, 'You find that boy, and when you do, you make it up with him. You two need each other.'

It was the only vaguely sentimental thing that Alexa had ever heard from the ancient sorceress.

And now she sat on her own attempting to put the old woman's plan into action.

In her mind she pictured the spells as two separate entities, each unique and individual for now. She needed to give them some imaginary form for what she was going to attempt, so she settled on animals, conjuring up the image of a blood-red fox for the location spell, while the thought transfer magic took the form of a bright blue monkey. These creatures were indistinct and ethereal to begin with, little more than vague coloured outlines, but as Alexa intoned the archaic words and sounds necessary to cast the spells, they took on a more 'solid' form inside her head. She hadn't even begun the difficult part, and already her head was swimming with the effort of holding two spells together in her mind.

She sensed the heat generated by the thought transfer spell, and regretted not changing into something lighter and more comfortable before starting. In addition, she was aware that the empty ceramic mug she'd placed on the coffee table before her had begun to shake and jitter on the glass top, making a harsh staccato noise. As quickly as they'd come, Alexa pushed these thoughts away, knowing that she must block everything else out if she was going to succeed with her plans.

She took a deep breath, pulling the air in through her nostrils and slowly expelling it through her mouth as she began the complicated task of merging the spells. She imagined the two spells becoming one, folding the energies and structures into each other. In her mind's eye she watched the blue monkey approach the fox cautiously, only to be driven back as the other animal snapped at it aggressively. The monkey skittered away, its eyes never leaving its crimson adversary. It came again, drawing the fox towards it, but this time, as the fox lunged at it, the monkey rose up on to its back legs and leaped into the air, coming down squarely on the fox's back. It wrapped its back legs around the other creature's middle and adopted a stranglehold around the fox's neck with its forelimbs. The fox turned its head this way and that trying to bite the monkey, but its simian foe was not to be thwarted. The monkey hung on, never relinquishing its grip on the fox's neck, until the macabre dance became progressively slower and slower and the fox finally came to a halt. The two creatures began to blend into each other, their colours and features merging and morphing until eventually all that was left was a freakish purple hybrid.

A film of sweat covered Alexa from head to toe, and she could feel a bead of it snaking its way down her spine as she sat bolt upright on the sofa. The heat was intense, as if she were sitting directly in front of a huge blazing fire. In addition, it was obvious that it was no longer just the mug that had taken on a life of its own. Even with her eyes firmly closed, she sensed that a number of previously inanimate objects were in orbit in the air all around her. Indeed, the air itself crackled and hummed with energy, adding to the discomfort and apprehension she was feeling. But all of these things occurred to her as if the thoughts belonged to another person – as if she were not really occupying her own body any more.

The purple fox-monkey-thing was eager to be put to use. It ran around in tight little circles or jumped about wildly, and Alexa knew that she couldn't contain it for much longer – not without undoing all of her hard work. So she concentrated one last time and sent the thing out – set the spell free of her body and mind, and loose into the world beyond where it had but one job: to find Trey Laporte.

Alexa's mind and body were suddenly reunited. She felt herself become whole again, and with this sensation came a great wave of exhaustion which elicited an unexpected gasp from her. She opened her eyes and looked about her at the chaos she had created.

The apartment looked as if it had been at the epicentre of some terrible earthquake, either that or a tornado had ravaged the room. Charred furniture was tossed all about the place, ornaments were smashed, curtains torn from their poles. The smoked glass coffee table had a huge crack in it, and there were ugly black and grey scorch marks in the thick white carpet. The leather sofa beneath her was scorched too, and she let out a little whistle as she realized that she herself was completely untouched. Still, Alexa dreaded to think what her father would say when he saw the damage. She froze then, her heart sinking a little at this last thought. She knew there was a good chance that her father might never get the opportunity to see the inside of the apartment, or anywhere else for that matter, ever again, and this thought brought with it a deep despair which she knew, should she give in to it, could be the undoing of her.

She was so very tired.

She tried to fix her thoughts on the spell, but it was impossible. She was close to utter exhaustion, and could hardly hold her head up any longer. Despite her attempts to keep them open, she could feel her eyes begin to close. She whimpered a little, hating the loss of control, but had to give in finally. Her eyelids came down like shutters, and she slumped over to one side.

Within moments she was fast asleep.

17

Alexa urged herself to move. She could hear the rasping breath of the thing behind her. It was travelling quickly, and would be upon her any second. But her feet were rooted to the spot. She tried to turn to get a look at whatever it was that was bearing down on her, but she couldn't – her head, like her legs, refused to obey her commands, and she was forced to stare straight ahead.

It was almost upon her. She could feel the heat coming from its body and sense the dark malevolence it directed towards her.

In that dream place, somewhere between deep sleep and waking, Alexa frowned. She could feel the soft leather of the sofa beneath her cheek, and she knew exactly where she was. The nightmarish scene and the fear that came with it began to fade. She kept her eyes closed and concentrated on holding on to the images. Because the terror had not been hers, it had been Trey's. She was seeing these things through him, and she had to try and maintain that bond somehow.

Trey?

She reached out to him, holding on to the tiny thread that linked the two of them now that the locating spell had found him. She concentrated hard on that connection, aware that it could break at any moment.

Trey, it's me, Alexa.

There was no response. A blank nothingness greeted her. Had her spells worked properly?

Trey. Please talk to me.

She waited, and was about to try again, when she sensed something reaching back out to her. She concentrated.

Alexa?

She held on to that small voice, focusing all of her efforts on maintaining the link with it.

Yes, Trey. It's me.

A series of patterns and colours, most of which were dark and sinister, formed in her mind's eye: jagged, hard lines against blacks and greys. But there was something else, something brighter behind the harsh forms, and she sensed that Trey was unwilling to believe she was with him in case it proved to be another trick played on him by the hallucinations he was obviously suffering from.

It really *is me. You are* not *imagining this. I'm trying to find you. Are you OK?*

Strange images popped into her mind. Images of werewolves running through a vast forest, hunting together as a pack. An image of her as she'd looked when they'd met that first time after her father had rescued him from death in the care home and brought him back to London. A man who, judging from the resemblance to Trey, must

118

have been his father, stood looking back at her, flames licking at his skin as he did so. And then the terrifying image of Caliban filled her head, and it was as much as she could do not to sever the connection between the two of them as the vampire opened his mouth impossibly wide and lunged towards her with those terrible fangs.

She forced herself to remain calm, and tried to help Trey do the same by pushing reassuring thoughts and images back along the connection in Trey's direction.

Where are you?

Another jumbled and chaotic series of images flashed through her mind's eye.

Trey, I need you to concentrate. Please. I need you to give me some clue as to where you are.

She was back in the forest. Thousands of identical trees surrounded her on all sides. They seemed unending. Everything was still under the dark canopy. And then out of the woods came a huge white wolf, its cobalt blue eyes standing out in stark contrast against the sea of brown and green all around.

Alexa knew who the wolf was. She'd seen those eyes before.

Where, Trey? Where has she got you?

The forest disappeared and she was standing on a London street. A black taxi cab drew up alongside her. It was packed full of nether-creatures: demons and djinn of all sorts filled every inch of the interior, their faces jammed up against the glass as they stared out at her. And suddenly she was in the midst of them. Sitting on the floor of the cab, their faces and hands and legs and bodies all pressed against her. The noise was terrible as they screamed and wailed and gnashed their teeth.

The taxi stopped suddenly and the back door flew open. The demons poured out of the vehicle like a thick and viscous liquid, dragging her along with them as they spilt out on to the ground, jabbering and screaming at the top of their lungs.

She looked about her, trying to make sense of what she was seeing against the chaotic images. There was a dilapidated old building up ahead, neglected and disintegrating under the rust that attacked it from all sides but there was little to distinguish it from thousands of others that must exist in the city.

Then the sign caught her eye. It was difficult to see at first, the metal it had been printed on having suffered the same fate as the walls on which it was mounted. But there was a name there: *Caulden & Son Ltd.*

The scene went black.

Hold on, Trey. I'm coming for you.

Alexa broke the connection between them. She sat up, and winced at the thumping pain that the movement set off in her head.

She needed to drink. She was terribly dehydrated and felt even weaker than when she had first given in to the exhaustion earlier, but she pulled herself to her feet and made her way over to the kitchen. In spite of everything a small smile touched the edges of her mouth.

She had the clue she needed to find Trey and the werewolf bitch who was holding him against his will.

18

It had only been moments since the huge sonic boom, accompanied by the shockwave, had spread outward from the dark tower. Robert Holt was still by the burger van, down on his haunches, hugging his son to him and telling the boy that everything was going to be all right. He could hear the doubt in his own voice.

The air was filled with the sounds of screaming and yelling. Somebody was shouting in a loud voice for people to remain calm, but the advice wasn't being heeded. A small child was crying somewhere in the crowd, its high-pitched, plaintive wails rising above the rest of the noise.

'What the hell is going on?' somebody yelled in a voice filled with anger and fear. The question was echoed by others. 'Do something!' another added. Robert stood to look for the source of the noise. Two police officers off to his right were surrounded by an angry mob of people demanding to know what was happening. Both of the officers were thumbing the buttons on the side of their radios, shouting out for somebody, anybody, to answer. Behind them another policewoman on horseback was doing the same.

Robert took his mobile phone out of his pocket and

frowned at the blank screen. It was fully charged – he'd made sure of that before he left the house this morning – but the thing appeared now to be completely dead. He glanced about him, noting how the illuminated shop signs were all out, the interiors of those premises that had stayed open on the match day also dark. He glanced at the police again. The disbelieving look on their faces matched that of everyone else around them; nobody had any idea what to do, Robert was sure about that. The other thing he *was* sure about was that this . . . thing, whatever it was, posed an immediate threat to him and his son. He cast his eyes about him at the crowd, surprised at the number of people who were simply standing gawking up at the tower and the purple sky, albeit with a wide-eyed look of astonishment and horror.

Making his mind up, he stood and took his son's hand firmly in his own.

'Come on,' he said. 'We need to get out of here.'

Jake nodded up at him, and they began to make their way through the onlookers. Others had had the same idea, and they fought their way through the crowd together, heading back in the direction they'd come. Despite the congestion, they made surprisingly good progress. Robert had been an amateur boxer in his youth – a heavyweight – and his size and appearance meant that although he got a few looks from the people he manhandled out of the way, few actually said anything.

'Look!' a woman in the crowd suddenly shouted,

pointing at the base of the tower which was now about forty metres behind them.

At the sound of the woman's voice Robert glanced back over his shoulder and caught sight of what she'd seen.

In the midst of the mass of solid black rock, a large, rectangular area was 'shimmering', as if the very molecules which held the stone together were becoming dislodged, changing from a solid to something more akin to a liquid. His inner voice told Robert that whatever was happening, it was bad, and he redoubled his efforts to get through the crowds, raising his voice and ordering people to allow him and his son through.

He could tell that some of those around him had not witnessed the actual arrival of the tower, missing its appearance until now, as they walked towards the stadium up the Fulham Road. A woman to Robert's right turned to her husband, a wide-eyed look of amazement on her face.

'Do you think it's an alien invasion?' she said.

'Don't be stupid,' he growled back at her. 'It's some kind of stunt. That rich Russian owner's cooked it up. You watch – it'll turn out to be some kind of advertising thing.'

'But look at the size of it!' she said.

'It's a trick, I tell you. Mirrors or something!'

'I dunno . . .'

There was a sudden push of people from Robert's right and his hand was wrenched clear of Jake's. He stumbled to one side a little, only just managing to stay on his feet. He turned, bellowing his son's name, a gut-twisting panic

124

gripping him as he realized Jake might have fallen. He was a good head taller than most of those around him, but he could not make out where Jake was.

'Dad!'

He heard his son's voice calling him from somewhere off to his left, and he dived through the crowd, wrenching and pulling at those around him in his panic to get to his boy. And then suddenly there he was. Jake had sensibly grabbed hold of a concrete rubbish bin set into the pavement, and was clinging on to it.

Robert bent down and picked the youngster up.

'Put me down, Dad. I'm too heavy for you to carry.'

Robert ignored the boy and the pain in his back as he straightened up. He turned his head to glance again at the door that had appeared in the citadel's black stone wall. Because it was a door. It was no longer in its liquid form, it was a black, gaping maw now, and some of the people right at the front of the crowd had gingerly crept forward to peer into the darkness, to see if they could make out what lay within.

Robert heard the first scream before the creatures appeared.

Then he saw them.

He gasped, pulling Jake's head into his shoulder to block out any view the child might have of the things that charged out of the gap.

That they were zombies, he had little doubt. Even from this distance he knew nothing could have survived the terrible wounds those creatures had suffered and still be alive in any conventional sense. Both appeared to have had their throats torn out; long ragged ribbons of flesh hung down below their chins and flapped about as they ran. The undead creature that had once been a man also had a huge gaping hole in his face. But no blood came from the wounds. Robert was surprised how quickly they moved. None of the shambling and shuffling stuff of movies – these creatures tore into the crowd before them, biting and slashing and rending anything in their path, often grabbing on to the next victim and pulling them into a deadly embrace even before the last one was dead.

Thankful that he and Jake had got a head start on most of the crowd, Robert pressed on. But everyone was running now. The mass of people had transformed from fascinated onlookers to panic-stricken escapees in the blink of an eye, and were charging about in every direction, desperate to get away. Some dragged those in front of them back so that they could take their place, and many fell beneath the feet of the stampeding horde, their screams echoing those of the unfortunates already in the zombies' clutches.

Robert tried to push his legs faster, but the weight of his son in his arms stopped him. As if sensing this, Jake shook his head free from beneath his father's hand and looked up at him. 'I can run,' he said. 'Put me down. Please!'

Robert nodded, and lowered the boy to the floor. The crowd was streaming past them now, and they were both almost knocked over again as they stood in its tide. They held hands once more, and Robert saw an unexpected look on the boy's face: that of determination.

They set off, keeping a tight grip on each other.

They ran straight up the centre of the road, pumping their legs and gasping for breath as the adrenalin coursed through their bloodstream. But when they caught sight of what lay ahead, they slowed, as those around them had done, staring in disbelief. They watched as the fastest runners, those who had got way ahead of the rest of the crowd, went crashing into what could only be some sort of invisible barrier. They ran headlong into it and stuck for a moment, their bodies jerking violently as if struck by a lightning bolt, before being thrown backwards to the ground where they then lay, unmoving. Robert could see this happening across the width of the road and pavement. Looking to his right, up an arterial road, he could see the same thing happening – people slamming into an unseen barricade, only to be forcefully thrown back to the concrete as lifeless mannequins.

'What's going on, Dad?' Jake asked, the terror in his voice causing it to go up in pitch so that the boy screamed the question at his father.

Robert snapped his attention straight ahead again as he caught sight of a police van speeding up the road towards them. Its blue lights were on, but it occurred to Robert that he could not hear the engine or the sound of the tyres or, indeed, the siren he was certain would be accompanying those flashing bulbs.

The driver was gesticulating out of the front window for the people inside the invisible barrier to get out of the way, and sure enough a number did so, grabbing and pulling at those nearest to them to make a path for the vehicle to pass through. The route clear, the police vehicle sped up, and Robert watched as it came to the point in the road where the force field – for he was convinced that was what it must be – separated the two sides. He instinctively ducked as the van crashed into the invisible wall, its front caving inward under the impact, its occupants jolted sickeningly forward against their seat belts as airbags exploded.

There was no sound from the crash. The only noise that came to Robert's ears was that of the screams and shouts all around him as people realized they were trapped. Trapped inside an invisible barrier. With zombies.

He felt Jake tugging at his hand, and looked down at the boy. His son pointed off to his left. A man was standing in a shop doorway no more than three metres away. He beckoned at them, silently urging them to hurry. They ran in his direction.

'Come in, come in,' he said, looking over their shoulders at the sea of people. 'Quickly!'

They glanced at each other for a moment before stepping inside. As soon as they'd passed him, the old man quickly closed the door, throwing two bolts, top and bottom, to lock it. The inside of the door had a protective metal mesh covering the glass.

'I couldn't leave you out there,' the man said, turning to

them. He had a long measuring tape draped round his neck, and one brief glance at the interior confirmed to Robert that they were inside a tailor's shop. 'Not with a youngster, I couldn't.' He looked out through the glass pane of the door again before pulling a curtain across. He turned to face them.

'I've been through it all before,' he said.

'I'm sorry?' Robert managed. 'Been through what?'

'The war. The Nazis! That's what they are, these hooligans: Nazis!' He shook his head and sighed. 'They've smashed my shop windows up on more than one occasion. That was in the bad old days, when they were everywhere. Great gangs of them fighting in the streets. Skinheads in jackboots.' He looked at Jake and nodded his head as if to insist that he was speaking the truth. 'Now it looks like they're back.'

'You need to let more of those people in!' Jake said, not understanding what the old man was going on about. 'They're in danger!'

'No!' the old man said. 'If they want to beat each other senseless, let them. I just didn't want a youngster like you caught up in it.'

'It's not hooliganism,' Robert said, surprised at the calm in his own voice.

'What?'

'Didn't you see the thing?' Jake said. 'The tower?'

'Tower? What tower?'

Robert realized that the shop must have been shut, the

man working behind his curtained window when the black citadel had arrived. He quickly took stock of their situation, glancing down with concern at his son who kept looking towards the door every time he heard a scream or shout outside.

'OK,' he said. 'We should keep the door shut—'

'But, Dad! Those people out there—'

'Sit down, Jake,' his father said, nodding towards a red leather sofa by the far wall. The boy reluctantly did so.

'Mr – ?' Robert nodded at the old man, offering his hand.

'Lipman. Benjamin Lipman.'

'Thank you for letting us in, Mr Lipman. Now I think you should sit down too.' He gestured for the old man to join his son on the sofa. 'I need to tell you what's really going on out there.'

19

Caliban stood looking out at the scenes of chaos unravelling before him, the sounds of terrified screams reaching him from the streets below. The death toll was already more than satisfactory, and he'd been surprised at the carnage just two of Helde's creatures had caused in such a short period of time. He'd watched as the zombies charged into the crowd, killing and maiming everything before them. They were insatiable and moved with incredible speed over short distances. The immediate area in front of the tower was now littered with dead bodies. Bodies which would not stay dead for long.

He'd been amused at the ineffectual attempts of the police to deal with the situation. Cut off from all communications outside the dome, they'd had to act on their own initiative. A mounted officer had charged at one of the revenants, the horse smashing the zombie to the ground where its hoofs had crushed the creature. Caliban had watched, a smile on his face, as the police officer had first reined the horse to a halt, then wheeled it about, only to shout out in horror at the sight of the mangled zombie getting back to its feet. He spurred the horse forward again, but this time the undead creature was ready for him. It leaped up, hooked an arm round the officer's waist and dragged him out of the saddle. Moments later, the policeman's screams were abruptly cut short.

The sight of all the blood was igniting the vampire's own desires, and he could feel the irresistible urge to go out and hunt.

Trying to take his mind off his own hunger, he gazed out at those humans he could see gathered at the limits of the impenetrable Shield that Helde was maintaining around them. Many of them still flung themselves against the invisible wall, despite having seen others' excruciating attempts to escape in the same way.

The dome of protection was not as big as he'd wanted; Helde had felt it prudent to keep the radius much shorter than they'd originally planned, arguing with him that it was better to have a smaller, stronger Shield than one which extended further but was less stable and prone to breaches from the outside.

'And the zombies will find it easier to track down prey that escape the initial attacks,' she also pointed out.

The plan was to wait until the zombies' victims started to reanimate, recapture the nearest few, and then simply move the tower on, leaving his brother to deal with the carnage left in their wake. Helde would need a short period in which to recuperate, but there were many places they could move Leroth to that were far enough away from his brother's forces to give them the time they needed. Then they could repeat the process over and over again in different locations, moving in and out quickly, and wreaking havoc anywhere and everywhere without the need to endanger themselves too much.

He had to admit, it was a brilliant plan. The zombie plague would spread like wildfire. Merely releasing two revenants had resulted in the wounding or death of at least fifty humans so far, and soon these would reawaken and begin to attack for themselves. When that happened, the Shield would not be here to contain them any longer and the spread would be fantastic: fifty would quickly turn into hundreds, hundreds into thousands, until in no time there would be a zombie army on the march with no one left to stop it. Even his brother – and his werewolf sidekick – could not fight a whole zombie army, legend or no legend. Then he would put into place the second part of his plan: setting up prison camps of captured surviving humans that he and his kind could feed from – battery farms in which the vampires would breed an inexhaustible supply of food.

He turned to look at Helde who was slumped on his throne, her eyes closed, mouth moving silently.

He'd assured the sorceress that he would not leave her while she was in this state. The concentration and effort needed to perform the magic was immense, requiring her to take her mind into another plane, leaving her weak and wholly vulnerable to attack.

But the smell of blood wafting up from below was too much. The vampire closed his eyes, imagining how quick and easy the hunt would be right now. He'd only be gone a matter of moments, and if necessary he could bring his victim back here to feed – a takeaway. Besides, no one could penetrate the Shield or would dare to enter Leroth!

He nodded to himself, having made up his mind.

'Back soon,' he said to the sorceress, blowing her a kiss.

He turned and went out of the room, leaving her alone with the lengthening shadows.

20

Alexa took the elevator all the way down to the underground car park beneath her father's building. As she stepped out of the lift doors, she looked about her to check that there was nobody around. There were closed-circuit TV cameras trained on every inch of the space, but she'd prepared a little diversion in the security guards' office that monitored the feed, so that right now they should be more concerned with the foul-smelling black sludge rising up from the floor. She only needed them to be distracted for a minute or so.

She ran across the cold concrete floor and up the exit ramp. There was one final guard she needed to avoid, but she knew there was a good chance Harry, who sat in the small hut by the car park barrier at the top of the ramp, would be less than vigilant. Sure enough, she peered round the corner to see him with his head buried in a newspaper. She walked silently past the hut without disturbing him. Alexa allowed herself a smile; she'd slipped out in this way on a number of occasions in the past, and good old Harry had never once caught her out.

In the street above, she crossed the road, hailing down the first black taxi cab that came her way. She climbed into the back of the vehicle and sighed with relief. Her father had endorsed her mission to find and help Trey, but he'd assigned two Maug demons to go with her for protection. The last thing she wanted was a couple of great lumbering bodyguards getting in the way of what she had to do, so she'd elected to go it alone and sneak out undetected.

'Where to, miss?' the cabbie asked over his shoulder.

'I'm not absolutely sure yet,' she said. 'If you could just head towards Tower Bridge, I'll let you know as we go.'

The cabbie puffed out his cheeks and was about to say something when Alexa waved two twenty-pound notes at him in the rear-view mirror.

'You're the boss,' he said and pulled away from the curb.

Her attempts to find a listing for Caulden & Son Ltd – the name on the sign Trey had shown her – had drawn a blank, so she'd resigned herself to finding him the hard way. When she'd reached out to him before, the link between them had been metaphysical in nature – a merging of minds. But now she had an image of the physical space he was being held in to concentrate on she knew she'd be able to translate that link into an actual path. She could already sense that they were going in the right direction. It was like water-divining with those dowsing rods that crossed when the person carrying them walked over an underground spring or well. As long as she kept her mind free of any distractions, and pictured nothing but the dilapidated building and that rusty sign, she could *feel* the route she had to navigate through the streets. Each time they went past a turning that she realized they should have taken she told the driver to stop and turn back, eliciting loud moans and groans from the disgruntled cabbie, who was no doubt keen to get rid of his eccentric passenger.

She realized that beyond *finding* Trey, she really didn't have much of a plan. Initially she'd assumed that Ella alone had taken Trey, but the more she thought about this, the less it seemed likely. Alexa shook her head, forcing these concerns away. She'd simply have to deal with whatever and whoever was responsible for Trey's capture when it came to it.

'Take this left,' she said suddenly to the driver, causing him to turn quickly and eliciting a screech of protest from the rubber tyres.

'Look, miss. I'm not bein' funny or nothing, but I've had just about—'

'Shh!' Alexa commanded.

She was near now, she could sense it, and she barked out the next few directions to the driver before they were even at the junctions, forcing him to navigate a series of quick turns this way and that until they finally pulled into a street in which most of the houses were boarded up, and those that were not looked as if they should be. At the end of the road was the entrance to an industrial estate, and this too had the distinct appearance of being unused and derelict.

'Stop here,' she said. She shoved the two twenties at the

driver and climbed out. Behind her she heard the taxi turn around and quickly drive off.

The feeling that Trey was here was stronger than ever, and she knew that somewhere up ahead was a rusting old hulk of a building that had once belonged to Caulden & Son Ltd.

She strode forward, telling herself that no matter what happened she would not be leaving without Trey, and that whoever was responsible for abducting and drugging him would be sorry they ever laid eyes on the sorceress Alexa Charron.

21

Lucien, Hag and Tom got out of the car, the vampire doing so hesitantly, still fearful of the fiercely blazing sun overhead despite Hag's reassurances that he would be fine and didn't need the sunblock he'd smothered himself in. Nonetheless, his new ability to go out in the sun had arrived just in time for this, their biggest and potentially last great stand, and he was grateful for that. Lucien and his two colleagues stood side by side surveying the incongruity up ahead while they waited for the demons to join them from the other car. There were only a handful of them in all; Lucien had reasoned that taking a large number of demons through to the other side of the Shield could cause even greater panic and distress when they were revealed for what they truly were. For now they were still hidden behind their human disguises, but that would no longer be the case once they were inside. Besides, he needed his team back at the offices almost as much as he needed those by his side right now – if anything went wrong, they could be ready to react instantly.

The long line of traffic, coupled with the large number of people who now jammed the Fulham Road and every other street in the vicinity, made further progress by any other means than on foot impossible. But even from here, looking across the sea of heads before them, they could make out the Shield.

It looked like some kind of monstrous snow globe, but instead of tiny flakes of white plastic snow, this one was filled with a hazy fog that shifted and swirled behind the hemispherical barrier.

Tom gave a small whistle but said nothing.

The mood of the crowd seemed to be teetering between wonder, bafflement, shock and fear. It would not take much for those standing and staring in amazement to become a wild, panic-stricken stampede. Lucien could hear the speculation all about him – alien visitation, a stunt or a trick. One old man was brandishing a Bible at anyone who came within shouting distance, announcing gravely that this was the Judgement day, when they would be made to pay for their sins.

'We'll never get through this lot,' Tom said to Lucien, nodding at the vast crowd before them.

'We'll get through them,' his boss answered. 'Desperate times call for desperate measures. Come on,' he commanded, beginning to push his way forward. He could just make out the police cordon up ahead and he headed for it. Most people moved aside as the vampire politely but authoritatively asked them to make way; those who didn't were given a private viewing of Lucien's fangs. The time for hiding what he was had passed. Despite the fear and tension he was feeling, Tom had to smile at the sudden change in these individuals; at first aggressive or belligerent, they shrank back in horror after a single look from his terrifying boss. It was a crude but effective means of clearing a path.

Approaching the police barrier, Lucien moved his arm so that the huge bladed weapon that hung from his hand by a wrist strap was obscured under the long black leather coat he was wearing. The vampire glanced behind him to check that Tom, Hag and the demons he'd brought along were all still together. People were pushing forward towards the metal blockade, and the police, two deep in places, were having a tough time keeping them back. Some of those at the front clearly had family or friends who were at this very moment trapped inside the thing up ahead. Their angry and frightened questions were met with placating but ineffectual words from the baffled officers behind the metal cordons. Off to one side, several reporters were gathered, making frantic notes and phone calls – one of them even had a small camera crew with her and was trying to interview an awkward-looking policeman. Tom looked up to see a police helicopter hovering in the air above them, its rotors making an angry chugging sound over the crowd noise. Lucien had made his way to the far end of the barrier where it mounted the pavement, terminating at a shop front.

'You'll have to get back, sir!' a young policeman yelled in the vampire's direction as he stepped forward.

'I don't think so,' Lucien replied. 'You see, my friends and I need to get over there.' He nodded his bald head in the direction of the dome-shaped monstrosity in the near distance.

'That's impossible, sir. You'll have to go back.'

The vampire shook his head, and the young officer glanced to his right at his colleagues. The crowd in the centre had pushed forward again, and a number of the police were concentrating on coping with the surge. Lucien was faced with only four officers.

The vampire looked into the four men's eyes, taking in each one in turn. He felt their fear and insecurities, and he knew that they were as terrified of the thing at their backs as everyone else was. The vampire took a deep breath and *blinked*. For everyone in Lucien's immediate vicinity, the world stopped. It was as if time had been placed on pause, all sound and motion ceasing to be.

'My friends and I need to get past this barrier,' Lucien said in a low, urgent voice. 'You and your colleagues will allow us to do so. You will move aside long enough for us to get through, but you will not allow anyone else to pass. When we are behind you, you will forget that we were ever here. Do you understand?'

The police officers all mumbled that they did.

The vampire nodded, adding, 'You're doing an excellent job. Stay brave and keep these people here safe. We'll do what we can to get this thing sorted.'

The uniformed men all nodded.

'Good. Now move the barrier, please.'

They did as the vampire commanded, pulling it a little to one side so that Lucien's people could squeeze, single-file, through the gap. The vampire was the last to pass. 'That's all of us,' he whispered to the officer who'd first spoken to them. The policeman nodded and quickly dragged the metal barrier back in place. As soon as he did so, the world seemed to restart for the young constable. He frowned for a second before facing the angry crowd ahead of him again, yelling at them to calm down. He had the strange feeling that something or someone was behind him, and the thought sent a shiver down his spine. A large woman wearing a blue baseball cap stepped up to the barrier and began shouting in his face. He forgot his unease and concentrated on the task at hand – to keep these people away from whatever that weird dome thing was until the authorities could work out what they were going to do about it.

Lucien and his team hurried towards the Shield, leaving the worst of the noise and clamour behind them. As they drew nearer they could make out the vague figures of people on the other side. Ghostlike, they lined the perimeter, some hurrying up and down along its length looking for a means of escape, others frozen in despair. As they watched, a figure came into view, running through the others, and threw itself at the barrier. He or she – it was impossible to tell which – stuck there for a moment, jerking violently as if some huge electric current were flowing through their body, only to be forcefully flung backwards away from the wall again and into the mist behind.

It wasn't just those people on the inside of the Shield who had tried to breach its defences. All around there were wrecked cars and vans that had been used to try to find a way through. Most of them had come to a crashing halt at the perimeter of the shimmering force field, their front ends concertinaed and crumpled with the power of the impact.

There was a shout, and Lucien turned to his right to see two uniformed officers hurrying towards them.

'You lot! What are you doing here? This is a restricted—'

Hag mumbled something under her breath, and the men simply crumpled to the ground in an unconscious state.

'Go,' Lucien said, nodding to the two incubi demons he'd brought along. They hurried over to the fallen men, took one glance at them and transformed into their perfect replicas. They dragged the unconscious officers to the safety of an abandoned car where they quickly swapped into their official uniforms. This done, one of them came trotting back over to Lucien and the others.

'We'll go on patrol now and make sure you're not disturbed by anyone else.' The demon nodded at its boss.

'You're not to hurt anyone, do you understand?'

'Of course,' the demon said. 'Good luck,' it added before rejoining its partner.

Lucien nodded his appreciation to Hag. The team moved forward again until they were no more than a few metres from the Shield wall. Immediately before them was a vertical shimmering force that rose up to about the height of a bus before it began to curve away. The 'wall' stretched from one side of the street to the other, passing straight through buildings and continuing on the other side.

'Why's it so foggy in there?' Tom asked.

'It isn't,' Hag answered. 'The Shield just gives that impression. If you think what it was used for, it made sense to have the movements of troops within the cordon kept hidden from those on the outside. In there,' she said, pointing, 'the sky will be dark and purple and clear – a little piece of the Netherworld brought right here to Earth.'

'How big is it?'

'Big enough,' the sorceress said. 'I shudder to think how many people are trapped in there, or what might have happened to some of them already.'

There was a pause during which nobody said anything.

'Exactly how long is it since Leroth was first transported here?' Lucien asked.

'An hour and four minutes,' Tom said with a glance at his watch.

The vampire turned to look at Hag. 'How long does it take for a zombie's victim to reanimate? How long until those that have died in there come back to life?'

'That depends on the nature, and the outcome, of the attack. If the zombie has killed the person with a bite, the infection will quickly pass through the victim's body. In those cases the reanimation could take place in as little as an hour, maybe less. If the victim survives the attack, he or she is still infected, but it will take longer.'

Lucien frowned. 'So those killed in the first wave could reanimate at any time.'

'Great!' Tom said, swearing under his breath. 'We have

145

no idea how many zombies Caliban brought with him in the first place and now they're about to multiply by . . . well, we don't know how much!' He shook his head and pointed at the dome-like barrier. 'We could be facing anything from one to a thousand creatures when we go in there, Lucien.'

Tom looked down at the machete-like weapon in his hand. They'd all been issued with one, and he hoped it was going to be enough to stop whatever they encountered when they got on the other side of that wall. They were no ordinary blades: they were forged in the Netherworld from a special ore found only there and they were almost impossible to blunt. Even so, the Irishman wished that he were taking something a bit more *military* in with him – an Uzi or a Glock maybe. Even better, an M4 carbine with a tasty little 40mm grenade-launcher underneath – that'd suit him down to the ground. But guns, just like electrical equipment, simply failed to work in the Netherworld. No, this was going to be hand-to-hand combat, with all the gruesome horrors that entailed. He hefted the heavy blade in his hand and puffed out his cheeks. 'Well, I suppose we'd better get inside and see exactly what we're up against.'

Lucien turned to Hag. '*Can* you breach the Shield?' He was almost afraid to ask – their whole plan relied on the witch being able to do so, but it was no small task and not guaranteed by any means, however powerful she was.

Hag turned from her contemplation of the Netherworld-filled dome. 'I can,' she said simply.

Lucien inclined his head gratefully. 'And how long for?'

'It won't be easy. That Shield was the tower's greatest defence during the Demon Wars. It's big, bad magic and Helde's done a good job of getting it working again. But old Hag's got a few tricks up her sleeve. I'll get it opened long enough to let you and your team through, and back even – don't worry about that.'

'Could you hold a large section open longer than that?'

The old woman frowned.

Lucien gestured with his head in the direction of the shadowy figures on the other side of the Shield section closest to them. 'I want to get as many of those people out of there as we can.'

'What about zombies breaking out too?'

He shook his head. 'If there were any undead that close to those humans they'd have run by now. Besides, if any did get through we could pick them off. I'm afraid we'll also have to be on the alert for anyone bitten but unchanged as yet . . . we'll have to pick them off too . . .'

There was a long pause while everyone digested this.

'If I do as you ask,' Hag said eventually, 'and things go wrong for you inside, there'd be no possibility of you retreating to regroup. I'll be too exhausted to create an exit for you. You'd all be stuck in there with a load of murderous zombies unless either you can stop Helde or they move the tower and the Shield elsewhere.'

'That's what I'm worried about. If I'm right, my brother

147

plans to wreak havoc here then move on and do the same all over the world – we *have* to stop Helde here and now or it's all over, so I don't think we'll be retreating and regrouping, Hag. Come what may, I think this one is going to play out right to the bitter end.' He exchanged a heavy look with Tom, who gave a grim smile.

The old woman nodded. 'I'll get as many as I can out, but it's still going to be a drop in the ocean.'

'Thank you, sorceress.' Lucien turned to the rest of them. 'OK, let's go.'

22

'Wakey-wakey, sleepyhead.'

Trey mumbled something, shifting his body a little and causing the chains about him to clink and scrape against the concrete floor.

'Trey, wake up.'

He opened his eyes groggily to see Ella's face in front of his own. She was so close to him that he could feel her breath on his lips, and he threw himself away from her, his heart pounding. His head was still foggy, and he had the vague recollection of terrible dreams filled with terrifying creatures. There was something else, something about his dad . . . and Alexa, but it was all too jumbled and muddled up in his head.

'Have you thought about what I said the last time we spoke?' Ella said, standing up and looming over him.

Then it *did* all come back to him. The horror of Ella's revelation that Lucien and Alexa were dead at the hands of Caliban. Instantly he felt himself begin to unravel from the inside. Tears filled his eyes and snaked their way down his cheeks, and he realized that the sobs he could hear were his own. Alexa was dead. The person whom he cared about most in this world had been killed, and he'd been powerless to help her.

Because of Ella. Because of this insane person in front of him, the girl he loved was dead. And Lucien. If both Lucien and Alexa were gone, what about Tom? Were all his friends now dead? He groaned in utter despair. *Ella.* Ella had taken him away from the people he cherished when they'd needed him most.

'Are you listening to me, Trey?'

Trey's voice was almost a whisper. 'When I get out of here, I am going to kill you. Do you understand that?'

'Kill me?' Ella gave a small laugh. 'Why would you do that?'

'Because of you, my friends are dead. I'd say that was a pretty good reason, wouldn't you?'

She frowned at him for a second as if she couldn't make out what he was saying.

'But that's set you free, don't you see? You're no longer obligated to them. Now we can go forward, reform the Pack and—'

'You really are insane, aren't you?' He shook his head and let out a short derisive snort like a bark. When he spoke again his voice had a hard, hateful edge to it. 'It's funny, I always thought madness took a bit longer to take hold, but you seem to have gone completely nuts in no time at all.'

'Don't talk to me like that. Listen—'

'No! You listen to me, you crackpot!' His voice caught in his throat, his emotions running so high he could barely think straight. 'I hate you. Do you understand that? I felt sorry for you for a while back there – for what happened to your parents. What you did. And it's obviously tipped you over the edge.' He stopped and took a deep breath, doing his best to control himself. It would not do to Change right now because of a loss of control. If he did that he would become the kind of werewolf Ella had been when she killed her own parents. He needed to be thinking straight if he was to escape and exact his revenge upon her. 'I am truly sorry about that,' he continued more quietly. 'But I'll never forgive you for what you've done now.'

'Trey, you're being—'

'Look at yourself, Ella! You have me chained up like a dog! Doesn't that strike you as even slightly ironic?' He was shouting now, his voice echoing about the walls. 'You want me to join you in starting up a new werewolf pack like the original LG78 that my uncle formed. But what happened to that, Ella? It went to hell! They started to in-fight – they became hunters and killers of humans, and those that tried to stop them were set upon by the rest of the Pack.' He glared at her. 'And what happened when your boyfriend, Jurgen, tried to form it all over again, huh? Have you forgotten how you got that ugly great scar on your arm? You are what you are because of him. Because he went crazy. Don't you get it? You can't control it. And don't think for a moment that you can.'

Ella went to say something, but stopped, her facial expression changing so that she matched his cold, hard stare.

'You controlled it,' she said.

'I had the amulet.'

Her blue eyes bored into his. Then she fished the silver chain from her pocket.

'You mean this amulet?'

Trey swallowed, ignoring the pain in his throat as he did so. The amulet had been his father's and his grandfather's before that, and now it was his only means of escape. The power and control it gave him would enable him to free himself and exact revenge on the person responsible for the deaths of Alexa and Lucien and Tom. After that, he didn't care what happened to him. He eyed it hungrily.

'Look at you,' she said mockingly. 'Look at how your eyes lit up when you saw this thing. Did you think it gone forever?' She held it up so that she could examine it properly, the small silver fist at the end of the chain swinging back and forth in front of her face. 'You see, I think this little bauble is what has made you into the lone wolf you've become. Because of this,' she tapped the amulet with the tip of her finger, 'you've turned your back on your own kind.' She looked over at him. 'It was given to you by the vampire, wasn't it?' She inclined her head, waiting for an answer. When none came she carried on. 'It's the thing that's stopping you from realizing that you are a pack animal. Without this, you'd have to join us, Trey. Join us, or live like your uncle did – a pathetic old hermit who locked himself away every full moon and dreamed of the times when he ran with the Pack.' She nodded to herself, her eyes staring off into the distance.

In that moment, Trey knew exactly what she was planning

to do. He cast his eyes about and saw the heavy hammer on the floor behind her.

'Ella, don't!' he shouted as she knelt and reached out for the tool. 'Please, Ella! You have no idea what you're doing.'

She held the hammer up over her shoulder, and Trey closed his eyes, unable to look.

Alexa pulled gently on the outer door. She froze, hissing slightly through her teeth as the hinges made a low, rusty groan. But when no shouts or running feet came, she slipped through the gap and let the door shut behind her. She stayed quite still, allowing her senses to take in everything around her. She could hear muffled voices off to her left. She crept forward, rounding the large counter, and approached the door that separated the reception area from what she guessed must be the garage workshop on the other side. There was another door to contend with, and she wondered if it would be as noisy as the outer one had been. The voices on the other side suddenly became louder. She heard Trey shout out in anger, only to be answered by an equally loud female voice.

Without another moment's hesitation, Alexa yanked the door open and stepped through.

She looked across the workshop to see Trey chained up in the centre of the room between two hydraulic car lifts. Blondie was kneeling in front of him, her back to Alexa. She had a hammer held high over her head. A shock of terror went through the sorceress as she realized she'd walked in on some bizarre ritual in which Trey was about to be bludgeoned to death. She summoned the first spell that came to mind – a bolt attack.

'If you swing that hammer, it'll be the last thing you ever do, Blondie.'

Trey's eyes snapped open and he looked for the source of the voice, hardly daring to believe his ears. Alexa stood in the doorway between the outer office and garage. A wave of euphoria tore through him, dispelling in seconds the extreme grief he'd felt only moments before. The steely look on the young sorceress's face told Trey everything he needed to know – she most certainly wasn't dead, and she hadn't come to the garage for an MOT.

Ella turned her head slowly and looked back over her shoulder at the raven-haired girl.

'What are you doing here? How did you find us?'

'Put the hammer *down*!'

The two girls stared at each other intensely.

'And what if I don't?' Ella said eventually.

Alexa's arm flew out from her side, her hand spread wide. The small silver ball of energy that shot from her palm streaked across the open space and struck Blondie's wrist, causing her to scream out in pain and drop the heavy metal tool, which fell to the ground with a metallic clang. Ella clutched her burned wrist to her chest and sank forward, hissing in pain.

154

'Then I'll make you,' Alexa said, inwardly congratulating herself on her aim. Not bad under pressure – even Hag would have approved.

The young sorceress stepped into the room, moving cautiously and scanning the shadows all about her. 'Are you all right, Trey?' she said without looking at him.

He could only stare at her in disbelief, his heart thumping against his chest, unable for the moment to speak. 'You're alive,' he finally managed.

'Last time I looked I was, yeah.' She glanced across at him. He looked awful. 'How many of them are there?' she asked, still peering about cautiously.

'She's on her own.'

Alexa stopped. She turned to look at Trey properly for the first time. His skin was a sickly pale colour, and he was covered in scratches and small bruises. His wrists and forearms looked particularly bad – deep lesions marked the areas where he'd strained and struggled against the manacles he'd been placed in. She did her best to lighten the mood.

'On her own?' She shook her head and moved towards him, a rueful smile on her lips. 'You really are something, you know that, Trey? Allowing yourself to be captured by the first blonde bimbo who bats her eyelashes at you. You're not safe to be let out on your own.' She smiled at him. 'No, I think from now on I'm going to have to keep you in my sights at all times.'

'That suits me just fine,' Trey answered, returning the grin despite his battered state.

Alexa shot a glance at Blondie, who was still on her knees, leaning forward over her injured hand. She was about to tell the girl to get up and unlock Trey when she saw her lower her head and slip something over it. Trey noticed the movement too, and his attention switched from Alexa to Ella. He cried out as he saw the silver links among the long blonde hair.

'Alexa, RUN!' he shouted.

He was too late. Ella rose to her feet, and Trey watched as the clothes she was wearing ripped apart and fell to the floor. Her body was already covered in thick white fur and she'd increased dramatically in both height and breadth. Her head snapped up, the wolf snout causing her face to distort and extend. She howled out in pain as fangs and claws erupted from fingers and mouth. The transformation took seconds, and before Alexa had time to react, the huge werewolf had turned and was glaring at her through terrifying blue eyes that promised nothing but death.

The white lycanthrope sprang forward with its head lowered and teeth bared. Alexa reacted by firing another bolt spell at the creature, hitting it in the chest where the fur turned black. The air filled with the acrid stench of burned hair. The lycanthrope howled in pain, but the wound did nothing to stop its relentless charge. It shot out a hand, fingers extended, claws ready to rip the sorceress apart. At the last second Alexa ducked, dropping her upper body forward and rolling beneath the attack. She vaguely heard Trey's shouts of alarm. She was back on her feet and turning to see where the white nether-creature was, when the air was forced from her lungs in one great 'Ungff!' The werewolf's shoulder hit her squarely in the solar plexus, and she stumbled backwards, her head connecting with the metal platform of the hydraulic ramp behind her and causing a bright starburst of pain to explode behind her eyes.

She turned her head to see a blur of white fur. Only her ingrained reactions saved her from having her face torn off by the she-werewolf's claws. She jerked her upper body away at the last second, feeling the air millimetres in front of her nose being cut through by those deadly talons as they narrowly missed her. Her head was painfully reunited with the metal structure of the ramp, and she shot her right foot out behind her to regain her balance, but there was nothing but empty space where the ground should have been. Alexa let out a startled cry and fell down into the pit beneath the metal structure that held the car, her ankle twisting painfully beneath her as she landed. She squinted up through the dark curtains threatening her vision to see the head of the white werewolf appear. There was a murderous look in the creature's eyes, its lips peeled back to reveal two rows of deadly-looking teeth in what Alexa guessed must be a smile. The black fog swooped in again as consciousness deserted her and left her to her fate. The last thought Alexa had before she passed out was relief that she wouldn't have to see the look of triumph in the lycanthrope's eyes when it finally dealt death to her.

23

Trey watched Ella twist about as Alexa rolled beneath the initial attack, pushing off from her powerful legs and diving forward to close the space between herself and the sorceress once more. The lycanthrope was too quick, too strong, and the outcome was all too obvious to Trey.

He cried out as the vast creature barrelled into the human's body, forcing Alexa to stumble backwards and crack her head.

The world slowed. He stared, transfixed with horror, as the white-furred monster shot out a hand, fingers hooked slightly so that the claws could inflict the killer blow.

He was dimly aware that the terrible noise in his ears was that of his own screams as he struggled against the cold steel that held him.

Then something snapped inside him, as if an electrical switch had been flipped in his brain, and he shuddered as the resulting current flowed into every cell of his body, filling him with power. He stood as much as he could, the chains still hampering his movements, and bellowed at Ella to stop. He Changed.

Trey fully expected to be forced back down on all fours. Without the amulet he would not take on his usual upright, bipedal werewolf form – the form Ella was now in – but that of the terrible four-legged nether-creature, the Wolfen. As a Wolfen, unable to control his killer instincts, he could be as much a danger to Alexa as Ella. But there was nothing he could do to stop it now.

A tidal wave of agony broke over him. He cried out with the exquisite pain of the Change, the sound that escaped him going from a boy's agonized scream to a werewolf's bellowing roar. His bones thickened and morphed into new shapes. Dense, hard muscles appeared where there were none before, and he was vaguely aware that the handcuffs on his wrists and ankles had broken apart beneath the strain. It was then that he realized he was still standing upright in the half man, half wolf form he had always taken on when wearing the amulet. *I'm not Wolfen,* he thought. His head was awash with conflicting ideas and notions, but he shoved these away as quickly as they'd come. Now wasn't the time. Reaching down, he took hold of the steel girdle round his waist, fixed to the chains that still anchored him to the floor. He let out another roar and wrenched it apart.

The howl, followed by the sound of shattered metal falling to the floor, was enough to distract the she-werewolf for a second. Ella turned just in time to see the grey-and-black lycanthrope leap forward, a deadly look on its face.

The two nether-creatures' bodies crashed together and they tumbled across the floor – claws tearing at haunches, teeth locked into flesh in a savage battle to overpower one another. Ella, in her werewolf form, was bigger than Trey –

159

more powerful and rangy. And he instinctively knew that this could only be used to her advantage if the fight broke up from an up close melee. Trey was a hardened combatant; he'd fought a number of opponents in this realm and the Netherworld, many of them much larger than him, and the difference in size did not intimidate him. But Ella too seemed to realize where her advantage lay – she wrestled out of Trey's grip and took a step backwards. Blood oozed from a bite wound on her shoulder, but Trey knew that the crimson gore smeared across her teeth and lips was his own. The pulsating pain in his forearm told him so.

Trey, his chest heaving, tried the thought-transfer spell he'd learned so that he could communicate when he was in his lycanthrope form. It came easily to him now, even in a dire situation like this.

Ella, stop this. You've lost your mind. You've—

The she-werewolf let out a snarl and lunged forward, shooting out a clawed hand. The blow was easily parried by Trey, who came in underneath the arm, raking a row of bloody claw marks across his opponent's belly that painted the surrounding white fur a dark crimson. But the move had left his head exposed for a moment, and his opponent took advantage of this, biting down into his ear and shaking her head to inflict the maximum amount of pain and damage. Trey howled but managed to force her away, and the two lycanthropes circled each other warily, both of them dripping coins of scarlet gore from their wounds on to the concrete floor.

The time for communication was clearly past. Trey put any thoughts of using the spell again out of his mind.

The werewolves' low growls and snarls reverberated back off the corrugated walls. Occasionally one of them would feint an attack, watching the reaction of their opponent, trying to pinpoint a weakness to exploit.

Gradually Trey moved away, manoeuvring himself closer to the pit beneath the car platform. As he passed close to it, he took a split-second glance down at the small, prostrate figure lying there. His eyes didn't leave his opponent for more than the time it takes to blink, but it was enough. The she-werewolf leaped forward, smashing into Trey, her weight and momentum causing him to fall backwards. It happened so quickly and she was upon him in a flash, her lips peeled back over her teeth, those great jaws stretched wide to deliver the killer bite. Trey was in a supine position, his legs caught up and compressed by the weight of the lycanthrope on top off him. He did the only thing left open to him: he pushed with all his might, forcing his legs outwards in a piston-like movement which sent his attacker sailing into the air. The white-furred lycanthrope crashed into the nearest of the hydraulic arms that held the platform up over the pit. Once strong, the equipment was now old and corroded, and the weight and force of the nether-creature smashing into it caused the fully extended arm to buckle, the metal shrieking in protest. There was a moment when nothing happened, and then the whole thing collapsed. The other hydraulic arm, incapable alone of supporting the immense weight of the platform with the car upon it, buckled like its twin, causing the entire structure to smash down at one end. Trey watched in horror as the white-furred werewolf lost her footing and fell into the front of the pit a split second before the car, unable to stay put on the acutely angled ramp, crashed down after her. A cacophony of smashing glass and shearing metal filled the air, and the garage was choked by a cloud of rust and dust, making it impossible to see.

Trey got to his feet and stumbled forward like a blind man until he came to the edge of the pit. His heart hammered as he peered through the slowly settling dust. The car was at a crazy angle – its front wheels still caught up on the platform, its rear end a mangled wreck in the bottom of the pit. Trey's stomach sank as he caught sight of a pale human leg sticking out from the wreckage. He quickly turned his head and peered into the other end of the trench. Another body lay there. This one had been saved by the hydraulic supports above it, which somehow managed not to give way as the opposite end of the structure had collapsed. But there was no telling how long that might last. The werewolf leaped down into the pit, where he gently took up Alexa and cradled her to him. A huge wave of relief flooded through the young lycanthrope as he felt the rhythmic beat of the girl's heart against his own chest. He jumped up out of the pit again and placed her on the floor.

She stirred, a frown touching her brow seconds before her eyes opened. If the sight of the giant seven-foot-tall werewolf bothered her, there was no sign of it on her face. Trey morphed back into his human form, amazing himself again with how easily he could bring about the transformation at will.

Alexa smiled and raised a hand, touching the flesh round his ear, which was a ruined mess.

'Are you OK?' she said.

'You came to rescue me. How could I not be OK?'

'Who ended up rescuing who?'

The teenager shrugged his shoulders and smiled down at her.

'Ella?' Alexa started to get up but fell back, hissing with pain.

The smile slipped from Trey's face.

'Just lie still for a moment, Lex. Can you do that for me?' She nodded and watched as he walked back towards the mangled mess behind him. He was naked, but if he was embarrassed in any way he didn't show it. He approached the far end of the pit, seemingly oblivious to the broken glass scattered about the floor at his feet, and lowered himself down into the wreckage.

Ella had been crushed, her body trapped beneath the car as it fell. He closed his eyes and hoped that she'd died quickly and not suffered in any way. He tried to forget what had happened in the last few days, remembering instead the girl he'd met in his uncle's house that first day, not so long ago, in Canada. She'd been a different person then – looking out for him when he'd run with the Pack, helping his uncle to find him when he was in peril, and ultimately making a great sacrifice by saving Trey's life when her lover, Jurgen, had tried to kill him.

He shook his head and climbed back out of the carnage.

On a hook by the main garage doors Trey spotted an old pair of overalls. They were filthy and more than a little moth-eaten, but right now the teenager had little choice. He took them down and stepped into them, buttoning the front as best he could.

When he walked back to Alexa she was on her feet, her mobile phone held to her ear.

'Taxi's on its way,' she said. She motioned with her head back in the direction he'd just come from. 'I'm sorry about your friend. Really, I am.'

Trey nodded. 'She wasn't always like that.' He frowned at her. 'How are you feeling?'

Alexa shrugged. 'I'm half vampire. I heal almost as quickly as you do.'

She reached out, pulling back the open front of the overalls to reveal his neck and chest, and placing her fingers there.

'The amulet? How did you—'

'It seems I don't need it any more.' As he said this he had a vague recollection of an old bearded man standing in front of him saying something important. He straightened up to his full height and when he spoke again, Alexa got the impression that he was doing so to himself as much as to her, as if affirming something. 'I'm the last hereditary werewolf. A son of Theiss.' He nodded, remembering. 'He came to see me and tried to tell me what I was and what I was capable of, but I wouldn't listen to him.'

'Trey—'

'But I'm ready now.'

'Good,' Alexa said slowly, a little spooked by Trey's behaviour – but there was something about him, a new confidence and assurance, that if anything she found . . . heartening. Especially in the circumstances. 'Because I think today's going to get a whole lot worse before it gets better.' She took his arm and steered him towards the exit. 'Come on, I'll explain everything in the cab.'

24

Hag had finished her preparations. She stood, shoulders hunched, staring at the floor. Her lank grey hair hung down in front of her face, obscuring it from the apprehensive glances cast in her direction by the others. Her eyes were open, but she no longer took in visual information of any kind. She was in another place now; her mind, her essence, had left her body and was in the realm it needed to be to perform the arduous sorcery ahead.

She could feel the huge power that existed in the Shield – a colossal thing of magic that seemed to have a life of its own now that it had been unleashed after all this time. And she sensed that it was aware of her too. Each time she reached out towards it with her own energy, she was forced to withdraw before it consumed her. She'd rarely experienced anything like it, and it frightened and thrilled her at the same time. Hag knew the effort that Helde must be expending to maintain the vast bulwark between the worlds, and the knowledge filled the sorceress with a newfound admiration for her adversary. She was still certain that the Shield could be breached, but it was going to be an awful lot harder than she'd first imagined.

The old sorceress readied herself again. Drawing upon

all of her considerable powers, she reached out to the vast force field once more, holding her nerve and merging with it for longer this time, its energy flowing through her own, filling her and making her one with it. For the first time she could sense the small changes occurring at a large number of points along the inner circumference of the dome. Quite sporadically, the Shield would concentrate its energies at these points, and Hag guessed what the cause was. She waited.

Lucien looked across at the old woman, who hadn't moved an inch since she'd gone into her trance. She stood, head down, one arm raised a little and bent at the elbow, forefinger slightly crooked, so that it appeared as if she was trying to remember something that was just beyond her mental grasp. He was momentarily distracted when, from the corner of his eye, he saw another trapped human throw themselves at the barrier. But this time the futile attempt had an effect on the sorceress. She flinched a little, the finger on that raised hand straightening so that it pointed straight up at the sky.

The vampire tensed, sensing that something was about to happen.

The sorceress looked up. Her eyes were open, but the globes which stared out from beneath the lids were devoid of any colour – black as coal, they stared sightlessly ahead.

'Now,' she said in a small voice, nodding once.

A tiny oblong, no bigger than a matchbox, appeared in the force field at the precise point where the human assailant had attacked it from the other side. It swelled for a second, doubling in size, before almost closing up again. Then quite suddenly it grew rapidly, expanding out in all directions until a large rectangular opening, big enough to drive a couple of cars through, appeared in the wall.

The shouts and cries of the people as they poured through the opening were sweet music to the vampire's ears. Lucien and the others sprang into action, bellowing at the escapees to hurry down the hill in the direction of the police cordon. Every face was etched with fear, and many of those fleeing clutched loved ones to them while glancing back over their shoulders to see if they were being pursued. These people had caught a glimpse of another world. A world full of nightmare and evil. A world that Lucien, and others like him, had fought so hard to keep from them, and he doubted that any of them would ever be the same again.

As if reading his friend's thoughts, Tom sidled over to the vampire, putting a hand on his shoulder and giving it a squeeze. 'At least you got these out,' he said. 'Many more are still going to be trapped inside when that breach in the Shield closes. And by the look of Hag, that won't be too long now.'

Lucien glanced across at the sorceress, and was taken aback by what he saw. She was shaking violently, her body convulsing as if she were being electrocuted in the same way that those on the other side of the Shield had been when in contact with it.

As if on cue, the walls of the rectangular opening began

to bow inward. No longer clean, strong lines, the edges of the rectangle were now undulating.

Those on the other side still trying to get through saw the same thing, and a sense of panic went through the remaining escapees.

Tom had taken up a position as close to the opening as possible, barking out orders for everyone to keep moving.

'This thing's going to close, Lucien!' he shouted back at the vampire. 'We need to get in there now, or we'll be of no use to those remaining trapped inside!'

Lucien nodded, but looked towards the opening again. Luckily, the initial stampede of people had lessened considerably, and those coming through now were people who had been further back from the outer circumference. At the sight of a means of escape these people had charged forward, sprinting for all they were worth up the road and from side streets so that they too might escape that hellish place.

'Just a few moments longer! We can still get more out!'

But as he spoke the breach suddenly contracted to about half its initial size. Lucien turned to look at Hag again. The convulsions that racked her body were worse than ever, and she was being thrown around on the spot like a rag doll, her arms and legs flying out in all directions.

'GO!' she screamed at him, her black eyes staring straight ahead of her. Small rivulets of blood ran from her nose and ears, droplets of the stuff spraying into the air as the spasms shook her. 'Go now before it's too late!'

Robert Holt peered out of a small gap in the curtains covering the windows and front door of Mr Lipman's tailor's shop. He'd been standing in the same position, staring out into the street for about an hour now. Earlier, Jake had been with him when they'd seen one of those zombies come down the road, people scattering in panic in every direction at the sight of the creature. Robert recognized it as the male he'd seen emerging from the black tower, but it was in considerably worse shape than it had been earlier. One arm hung uselessly down by its side, the bone which should have connected into the shoulder joint sticking out from its ruined clothing, and it dragged one leg along the ground as it shuffled up the road. For any living creature the pain would have been unbearable, but the undead zombie seemed not to notice. As they watched, the creature snarled and made as if to lurch towards the fleeing people who ran up both sides of the street, hugging the shops and restaurants. Robert sensed it was looking for something, its head slowly sweeping from side to side, milky, dead eyes seeking out its prey. Suddenly its head snapped towards a woman who was unable to run as quickly as the others – she was hobbling a little on an ankle that she must have twisted at some point. Like a lion spotting the weakest member of the herd, the zombie let out a terrible blood-chilling scream and loped off in the woman's direction. Despite its own injuries, it moved at terrifying speed.

She was not alone. Her husband or partner put himself

between the woman and the approaching monstrosity, making a last stand against this creature from hell. Those watching from the safety of the shop knew that it was a futile gesture.

'Go and sit down,' Robert told his son, pulling the curtains shut so that the boy would not have to witness what was about to happen.

'That thing . . .' Jake said, crying. 'That woman can't get away, can she? We're in here, safe, and she's stuck out there with that terrible . . . thing.'

The father sat next to his son on the red sofa. 'I know it's hard. And I wish you hadn't seen what just happened. But if we open that door and let them in we'll be putting ourselves in terrible danger.'

'We should do something!'

Mr Lipman came in from the door at the back of the shop. The old man had gone upstairs to see if his sick wife needed anything, having earlier explained that she'd recently come out of hospital and was still convalescing. He'd clearly heard their conversation. He walked over to the curtain to peer through the gap.

The man and the woman were both dead. They lay in a mangled heap on the floor, an island of wrecked flesh floating in a sea of red.

Mr Lipman turned and nodded at Jake. 'To keep yourself and those that you love safe is not cowardice, Jake.'

Earlier, when Robert had explained to the old man and his son everything he'd seen since the black tower arrived, the tailor had simply sat in silence, not interrupting once, even when Robert had told him about the two zombies.

Now Mr Lipman had seen it for himself. Robert took in the old man's reaction, and was surprised again at how calm and detached the tailor was.

'What are we going to do, Dad?' Jake asked.

The father took his son's hand. 'Someone will come and rescue us, don't worry.'

'They can't get in. You saw that police car!'

'Someone will come,' his father repeated.

The old man had sighed then, turned on his heel and walked back through the shop. After he'd left, Robert had taken up his position at the curtains, peering out through a tiny gap at the nightmare world on the other side. He'd stayed there, unmoving, until now.

Something caught Robert's eye. Something about the way the few people he could see at this end of the street were looking and pointing up the road, in the direction of the force field that he and Jake had seen earlier. Robert opened the curtains wider and stepped through the gap so that he could press his face up against the glass of the shop door. He strained to see what it was they'd been gesticulating at, and his frustration grew when he was unable to make anything out. There was something about the expressions on the survivors' faces. He turned to check he was not imagining things.

And there it was.

The look on their faces told Robert everything he needed

to know. Fear was replaced by hope, and that could only mean one thing surely – somehow the invisible barrier that they'd been trapped within had been breached.

'Wait here,' he said to his son, who, sensing the change in his father's mood, had come to stand by his side. He reached out for the bolts that secured the door from the inside.

'Don't go out there, Dad. Please!'

Robert dropped down on to his haunches so that his face was level with his son's. He smiled reassuringly. 'I won't be long. I just need to check something out. Wait here.' He straightened up and slid back the two heavy bolts. He paused for a second as he wrapped his fingers round the door handle, psyching himself up, before pulling it open and stepping outside.

He could already hear the change in the noise of the crowd – there were excited voices among the shouts. He walked out into that ghastly purple gloom again and looked to his left.

There was a huge opening in the wall at the end of the street where it straddled the shops on either side. The light coming in through the gap was bright and of an earthly hue that made Robert's heart jam up against his chest, so that it was as much as he could do not to cry out in joy. A deluge of people flooded through it. He could hear voices somewhere on the other side, directing the escapees to hurry up and giving them instructions about where they should go.

Other people in the street had also seen the breach. They

grabbed their loved ones, hauling them forward in a sprint to try and escape.

It took Robert less than a second to realize that this was his chance to get Jake to safety. He ducked back inside, shouting out to his son that they were leaving. He was already halfway across the shop, heading for the small glass-panelled doorway in the back that Mr Lipman had disappeared through, when he heard a shout of dismay from outside. There was something about that noise that spurred him on even faster. He took the stairs up to the apartment over the shop three at a time.

There was frosted glass door at the top. Robert pushed through it, hardly taking in the living room on the other side as he sought out the bedroom that Mr Lipman and his wife must be in. He was in luck: the first door he tried on the far wall opened on to a darkened room, the heavy curtains drawn against that terrible light outside. Lying in the bed was Mrs Lipman. One glance at the woman was enough to tell Robert that her husband had brought her home from hospital to die. Stick-thin, with hollowed cheeks and sunken eyes, she could have been one of those creatures roaming about outside. She didn't even look up as he came in. The tailor, who'd been sitting in a chair beside his wife's bedside, stood up, her hand still in his as he turned to face the intruder.

'We have to go,' Robert said, looking between them. 'I think we can get out.'

The old man slowly nodded his head as he took this in.

'We have to leave now. I don't know how long we've—'

'No,' the old man said. He smiled sadly down at the tiny figure in the bed next to him. 'My Rosa's not well enough to go anywhere.'

'I'll carry her,' the younger man said, taking a step into the room. 'Jake can hold your hand and I can carry Rosa. It's not far.'

The tailor cut him off with a shake of his head. 'No,' he said again.

Robert went to say something, but the sound of his son's voice on the stairs below stopped him from arguing any further.

'Dad!' Jake called up. 'There's something happening to that hole. It's . . . wobbling.'

Robert cursed himself for having left the front door open. How could he have been so *stupid*?

He glanced at Mr Lipman again. The old man had already stepped around the bed, and was shooing him out of the room. 'Go on,' he said. 'Get that boy of yours out of here.'

'Thank you,' the younger man nodded, grabbing hold of the tailor's hand and pumping it up and down. The old man waved him off, pushing him towards the doorway. Robert Holt stopped, turned and looked back at the frail old woman in the bed, her eyes still closed. 'Will you be OK?'

'We'll be fine,' the tailor said, gently shoving the other man out of the room and closing the door behind him. 'As

175

a boy I survived the Nazis. I'm sure we'll make it through this.'

Jake and Robert ran from the shop, the father dragging his son along behind him. The hole was significantly smaller than it had been when he'd first seen it from outside the shop, and with each step his heart sank as it continued to shrink. Whatever the exit was, it was clear it was becoming increasingly unstable and could shut at any second.

We're not going to make it! Robert thought.

Up ahead, a man threw himself at the breach. Robert watched, gasping as the gateway made another of those violent spasms just as the man dived towards it. The edge nearest to the escapee shifted dramatically and he plunged head first into the invisible barrier, screaming out as he convulsed wildly, before being thrown backwards to the ground, where he lay unmoving. At the sight of this, many of those running down the street cried out and faltered.

Robert and Jake were no more than ten metres or so away when they heard somebody shouting from the other side in a loud Irish accent, saying something about getting through to the other side before it was too late. This voice was answered by another that agreed, adding orders to grab their weapons and enter the hole immediately.

Father and son could now make out the people these voices belonged to through the gap: a tall bald man with the freakiest orange-gold eyes was throwing back one side of his coat, his fingers curling round the handle of the biggest knife Robert had ever seen. Another man, equally tall with close-cropped grey-and-black hair and an ugly scar on his face, was about to step through when he saw the father and son hurtling towards the hole.

'Wait!' he shouted in a broad Irish accent. 'There's a little lad and his dad coming.' He took in the two of them, his eyes narrowing for a second. 'Stand back and let them through!'

Something happened again to the hole. It closed for a moment, the healthy, hope-filled light that had come through it disappearing, replaced by that sickening purple colour. Robert cried out in anger and frustration. But the hole opened again. It was even smaller – no more than a metre across and two high – and the edges shifted to and fro.

'COME ON! You can make it!' Robert heard the Irishman shout. He could see him crouching down, peering through the gap at them and wildly urging them on with his arm.

Robert didn't hesitate. He strengthened his grip on Jake's hand and threw himself forward.

The humans tumbled through, landing in a heap on the tarmac road which greedily skinned the flesh from their hands and knees. Robert was aware of a high wailing sound and turned, realizing it was his son's voice. He pulled the boy to him and held him tight. He looked up at the late afternoon sky and thanked the gods for saving them both.

A shout from behind caused him to look back in the

direction from which they'd come. Time seemed to slow as a number of things happened at once.

The Irishman had gone through the gap followed by the tall bald man, who turned to look through the hole from the other side, his gaze resting for a moment on the father and son. In that terrible light his eyes, already a bizarre colour, seemed to glow with a fierce golden luminosity. He shifted his attention and called out to the three remaining men on the outside. As he did so, Robert noticed the vicious-looking fangs in his mouth.

A vampire, he thought. It was strange, but after everything else he'd experienced already that day, the sight of the creature did not fill him with the horror it should have.

The hole shrank, almost closed and opened again, and it was clear that it was at its most unstable. A female voice cried out, and Robert turned to look across at Hag for the first time, his mouth falling open at what he saw. She was not standing on the ground. Instead the old woman was suspended in the air about a metre above the road surface. The sight of a human levitating was shocking enough, but what was happening to the rest of her was truly horrifying. The old woman's body was being slammed around in the air, her head snapping back and forth, arms and legs flying out from her sides with a violence that was sickening. She looked like a life-sized marionette being controlled by a cruel puppet master intent on wrecking the toy.

He turned again to see that one of the remaining figures on this side had got through the breach in the wall. Jake whimpered in his arms, and his father clutched him closer. Despite the need to get his son to safety, Robert was incapable of tearing his eyes away from the scene unravelling before him. The old woman screamed out again, and as she did so Robert watched as the next man, hunched forward and carefully eyeing the shifting opening, made an attempt to get through to the other side, throwing himself at the hole which was now no bigger than the size of a car door. He dived just as the aperture closed for the last time. The old woman let out an almighty shriek and collapsed to the ground in a heap.

One half of the nether-creature fell to the floor on the human side, the other fell at the feet of Lucien Charron. There was no blood; the ghastly wounds on the severed body had been instantly cauterized by the awesome energy of the Shield. The air stank with the foul smell of burned flesh.

Lucien looked down at the severed head and torso of the demon, knowing that he was responsible for the creature's death. He lifted his eyes, meeting those of Tom, who gave a tiny shake of his head as if reading his thoughts.

'We should go,' the Irishman said, turning about and looking up the road.

They'd taken no more than a dozen steps when they heard a low groan from somewhere ahead of them. They stopped and watched as a woman – the same one that Robert had watched limping away from the zombie earlier – pulled herself from under the body of the man lying on top of her. That she was dead, or at least should have been, there was no doubt. Nothing could have survived the terrible wound on one side of her neck. Dull grey eyes, from which life no longer shone, stared out from a face devoid of any expression. She made a low, animalistic noise, something between a loud sigh and a groan, and slowly got to her feet.

'Ah crap,' Tom muttered.

The zombie's head snapped towards the sound, and she let out a blood-curdling cry as she took off, running down the road in the Irishman's direction.

'D'ya ever get the feeling that it's just going to be "one of those days"?' Tom shouted across at Lucien.

The man who'd been lying on top of the woman also began to stir.

'It looks like our fears have come true,' Lucien said, stepping forward and hefting the machete in his hand. 'They're reanimating already.'

Tom nodded, copying his boss's stance.

'Let's go to work,' he said.

25

Helde's spirit resided in a place of pure sorcery now. Her physical body was still at Leroth, but she was only vaguely aware of it. She'd had to immerse herself deeply in the dark magic necessary to maintain the Shield, and to do so she'd been forced to leave the body that her mind resided in. The otherworldly plane she now occupied was difficult and dangerous to inhabit for long. It was made up of complex, dark, interacting energies that were impossible to comprehend in any conventional sense, and she was forced to reinterpret them into something her mind *was* able to manage and handle.

She was the giant spider at the epicentre of a vast web that stretched out beneath her in every direction before it disappeared into the darkness on all sides. Strange and sinister things lurked in the inky blackness: things that would happily devour her if she allowed her concentration to slip. She could hear their low, guttural voices whispering to each other as they eyed her greedily. She had no right to be here – not for any length of time, anyway. Those adept in dark magic came to this place every time they used their skills, but it was usually a brief visit – a fleeting glimpse as they hooked into the energies here, and used them to conjure their magic. Each time it was different: a black forest, a subterranean cave, an inky underwater world – a thousand different variations. But the things *were always there, always waiting for a chance to feed.*

She was in control at the moment, but it would not do to let her guard down, even for a second.

She glanced at one of the strands she was crouched among. Thick black cords, the width of a man's arm, trembled and vibrated. They were fleshy and sticky to the touch, and beneath the pliant surface something squirmed and writhed as if the web were filled with living creatures, all of which were trying to find a way out through the labyrinth of threads. She stayed still, focusing her powers on maintaining the Shield and trying to ignore the malignant creatures pressing in on her from the void.

Helde sensed Hag before the old woman was anywhere near the protective dome that hung over Leroth. The sorceress was coming, and she was not alone. Helde knew that her adversary would try to breach the Shield, and that it would be up to her to stop that happening.

She felt the jangling pull at the edge of the web as Hag began to perform the magic she would use to try and create an opening. The vibrations along the threads of the web were transmitted to her body through long legs, covered in a vast array of hairs and sensors to pick up the tiniest of movements. It was in this way that she'd felt the ineffectual attempts of the trapped humans as they threw themselves at the Shield to try and escape. But this was quite different.

They had never met, but the moment Hag opened up her mind to begin the magic, the two sorceresses' energies became linked, and they knew and sensed things about each other, gaining an insight into one another's skills. Hag was an accomplished sorceress, and Helde knew how difficult it would be to try and hold the Shield completely in place in the face of her adversary's attempts to gain entry.

Helde's focus on the other sorceress was nearly her undoing. One of the shadow creatures seized its chance and lunged forward, pulling out of the darkness and swooping towards her, its mouth wide and teeth bared. She reacted just in time, bringing her magical defences back up to thwart the attack. At that moment a human threw itself at the supernatural barrier, and Hag used this and Helde's temporary distraction to redouble her efforts. Helde let out a shriek. She banished her dark attacker back to the shadows, but it was too late. Hag had found a way inside her defences and had created an opening in the Shield.

The great spider left its place at the centre of the web, scrabbling out in the direction of the wreckage that her adversary had caused. She quickly reached the site, taking in the ruined mess of the web, its perfect symmetry now in tatters. She began to spin new lengths of the black cord, pulling the stuff from the spinnerets at the back of her body and using all of her legs to weave it in and out, repairing the damage. It was hard work. Now that she'd breached the Shield, Hag fought to keep the hole open, and as fast as Helde wove her repairs, the old woman on the outside tore them apart again – a giant, invisible hand that smashed through time and time again.

Helde redoubled her efforts, spinning the black cords ever more quickly. She drew upon the dark energy that flowed from the source of the Shield deep in the bowels of the tower. It lent itself to her readily, bolstering her powers and making her stronger. At the same time she felt her adversary weaken a little. Spurred on by this, she repaired the wall again, and this time more of the patched areas held in place, the opening decreasing in size as the old woman tired. Helde allowed herself to reach out into Hag's mind again, and she felt the weakening sorceress's physical pain, her body ravaged by the counter-effects of the spell she performed. The old woman's agony drove Helde on even more, and then, quite suddenly, Hag gave in, her energies disappearing as she broke free from the dark realm and allowed the breach in the Shield to collapse in on itself.

Helde let out a hiss of triumph. She repaired the web again, and this time her construction held firm. She sank back, exhaustion eating its way through her, and as the enormity of what she still had to do dawned on her, she almost surrendered herself. But she could not let her master down. Caliban had brought her back to life. The vampire had fed her demon blood, then his own, to reanimate her. And now he stood guard over her while she was at her most vulnerable. She would fulfil her promises to him. She somehow dragged her bulky arachnoid body back along the black strands to the centre of the web, where she sank down, utterly spent.

184

26

Trey and Alexa stood outside the building that had been his prison, waiting for the taxi. They hadn't spoken since their last exchange, each lost in their own thoughts about what had happened and what was to come. They'd managed to clean Trey up a bit, using some old towels they'd found in the toilets at the back of the garage. He still looked pale and grubby, and the overalls he'd put on gave him the appearance of a prison inmate who'd escaped and was on the run. The cab driver must have had the same thought as he pulled up in front of them; staring out of the windscreen he gave Trey a less than friendly look.

They climbed into the back of the car.

'Chelsea football ground, please,' Alexa said.

The cabbie turned round in his seat and looked in disbelief at each of them in turn.

'You're joking, ain't ya? Haven't you heard? That part of the city is like a war zone now. Police, army, helicopters – I even heard on the radio that they're bringing tanks in. Tanks! In Chelsea! 'Ere, have a listen for yerself.' He pressed a button on the radio to increase the volume. A female reporter was in the middle of an outside broadcast.

'. . . *that the police have cordoned off the area*

surrounding the football ground, and are stopping anyone from returning to their houses and businesses for the foreseeable future. From my vantage point here on top of the shopping centre just off Fulham Broadway, I can see the vast dome-like structure that has got scientists and everyone else completely baffled. What is it, how did it get here, and what might its arrival mean to the people of London, the UK, and possibly the world?'

The broadcast switched back to the studio and a silky-voiced male presenter.

'Thank you, Anita. That's our reporter at the scene, Anita Harvey, and she'll be keeping us abreast of any developments that occur with regard to what many people are describing as the Dome of Doom. Please keep your calls, texts and emails coming in with your ideas on what the giant hemispherical object is, and we'll discuss them during the show.

'There's already been speculation that the thing is some sort of spaceship, and to discuss this possibility, and what it might mean to the human race if indeed it is an extra-terrestrial visitation, is Professor Daniel Linkwater of the University of St Andrews who is a member of the International Academy of Astronautics and of the SETI Permanent Study Group. Professor, what do you think the—'

'How close could you get us?' Alexa asked the driver.

'Look, I don't want to go anywhere near that thing, full stop.'

Alexa dug her purse out of her pocket and counted out

the money she had in it. 'I've got one hundred and fifty pounds here, and I can get another two hundred out of a cashpoint machine on the way.'

'Why are you so keen to—'

'My dad's inside.'

There was a silence in the cab as the driver considered this.

'How close can you get us?' Alexa repeated.

The cabby looked back at her in the rear-view mirror. 'Three hundred and fifty quid?' he asked.

Alexa nodded.

'Close enough,' he said, already pulling away.

The cabbie had informed them that he was sticking to the south side of the river for as long as possible, moving his way west before trying to cross the Thames as close to Chelsea as he could. He kept the radio on, scoffing at the views of some of the various experts and panellists filling the airwaves. He told Trey and Alexa that he was firmly of the view that it was an alien invasion, and that the people inside were all abductees who were going to be experimented on in some way.

'I saw this documentary about it,' he explained. '*They've* been watching us for years.'

Trey glanced across at Alexa, who was sitting completely motionless, head bowed slightly with her eyes fixed on the footwell in front of her. He caught snippets of the words she was whispering under her breath, words in a language that had no place in this world. He glanced up at the driver, who was looking back at him in the rearview mirror.

'You two are potty going up there. I know her dad's in that thing, but there's nothing you can do for him now. They've probably got him in a room somewhere, probes in every orifice, turning him into gawd-knows-what. Alien genetic manipulation,' he said in a low voice, then shouted at the driver of a car that pulled out in front of him without indicating. 'This is the first stage of an invasion. As soon as I drop you off, I'm going straight home. I'm gonna stock up on supplies, lock myself in my flat and wait this thing out. There's no way I'm going to be captured and experimented on by those bastards.'

He slowed to a stop at a red light.

As he pulled on the handbrake a low rattling sound started in the car. It got louder and more intense until Trey could feel the vibrations juddering through his body.

'What's that?' the driver shouted.

The purse that Alexa had put beside her as she'd got back in the car when they'd stopped for the cashpoint lifted off the seat a little, and Trey slammed his hand down on top of it.

'Maybe you've got a problem with your rear axle,' Trey said, cringing as he uttered the words. *A rattling axle? They were stationary!*

The small tree-shaped air freshener that hung from the rear-view mirror in the front of the car began to rotate back and forth, slowly at first, but picking up speed until it swivelled about the elastic cord it hung from at an incredible rate. The driver stared at it in horror for a moment, and whimpered. A staccato rat-a-tatting now filled the car. Every loose article, every gap and joint vibrated wildly. This, coupled with the hypnotic revolutions of the air freshener, was simply too much for the cabbie, who was already in a heightened state of fear and paranoia.

'They're coming!' he shouted, opening the door and piling out on to the road, almost falling under the wheels of an oncoming car.

'Wait!' Trey shouted, but the man was already off, running back up the street, shouting out warnings to pedestrians and looking up into the skies above as if he expected a beam of light to suck him into the mother ship at any second.

Quite suddenly the rattling stopped and the air freshener ceased its hypnotic swivelling.

'I know where they are,' Alexa said. 'Or at least I know where Hag is.'

'Great,' Trey said through clenched teeth, the muscles at the sides of his jaw bunching and unbunching as he stared at her.

Alexa took in his angry expression and then the empty front seat. 'Where'd he go?' she asked.

'Thanks to your witchy shenanigans, our cab driver has done a runner.' He motioned with his thumb over his shoulder. 'At this very moment he's legging it in that direction, telling everybody to do likewise because ET has come to eat them.'

'Oh.'

There was the sound of a car horn behind them. The lights had turned green again.

'You'll have to drive,' he said, nodding in the direction of the front seat.

'I can't drive! I've only had ten lessons.'

The car horn sounded again. Trey turned in his seat and gave what he hoped passed as a placating wave to the driver.

'Well, that's ten more than I've had. Look, we don't really have much choice right now. Besides, it can't be far, I saw a sign back there saying that football traffic should take the next bridge.' He nodded at the satnav attached to the front windscreen. 'Just follow that thing.'

Alexa went to say something, but stopped when the driver behind them sounded his horn for a third time and shouted something out of his window at them. Instead, she climbed over the seat into the front of the car. She pulled her seat belt on and adjusted the rear-view mirror. The engine was still running, so she pressed the clutch pedal, put the car into gear and took off the handbrake.

The car lurched forward sickeningly and stalled.

Alexa and Trey's eyes met in the mirror.

'One word,' she said threateningly. 'You just say one word about my driving, Laporte, and it could be the last one you *ever* say.'

Trey battled to wipe the smirk off his face.

Alexa restarted the car, put it in gear and drove off up the road.

27

'This is ridiculous!' Trey said, banging his fist down on the dashboard. He'd climbed into the front of the car and was now staring out at the vast line of unmoving traffic ahead of them.

At the far end of Battersea Bridge, in the direction they were heading, was a roadblock.

They'd been stationary for what seemed an age now, and they could just make out the line of metal barriers that the police had arranged across the road ahead of them. Male and female officers in bright fluorescent jackets were redirecting traffic down Embankment, away from Chelsea, and in the distance it was clear that similar barriers had been erected all along that route, stopping people from turning off and doubling back on themselves. The traffic was solid on this side of the bridge, but nothing was coming towards them on the other side of the road; it appeared the police had stopped that too.

Alexa slammed her palm into the steering wheel. 'What now?'

She watched Trey narrow his eyes and nod to himself, as if he'd decided on the only course of action left open to them.

'You're going to have to floor it,' he said.

'What?'

'Get this thing on to the other side of the road, and floor it.'

'Are you mad? They'll be after us in a shot! Look, see those things with bloody great engines and two wheels?' She pointed ahead. 'The ones with blue lights flashing on top of them? They're police bikes, and they're a sight faster and more agile than this old heap is going to be.'

Trey thumbed the screen of the satnav device hanging over the dashboard.

'We've only got to make one turn up ahead,' he said, decreasing the size of the map on the screen to show her what he meant. 'We go up Beaufort Street on the other side of that roadblock, and then left into Fulham Road. From there it's straight on until we hit Leroth.'

'They'll outrun us!'

'So what? They won't be able to pull us over, not on bikes. And by the time they've mobilized any cars to stop us we'll be close enough that it won't matter. We need to get there as soon as possible, Alexa, and it's either this or we get out now and try to make it all the way on foot.'

'They'll be armed.'

'Then you'd better drive quickly and make us difficult to hit.'

She looked at him for a second.

'I haven't even got a licence yet, and you want me to start a high-speed chase with the police.'

'If we don't help your father stop whatever is happening inside that Shield, I doubt not having a driving licence is going to be at the top of your list of troubles.'

She took a deep breath. 'I don't know why I listen to you, I really don't.' She took the handbrake off.

'That's my girl,' he said grinning back at her.

Alexa swung the wheel to move the car out on to the other carriageway and pressed the accelerator to the floor, crashing through the gears as she sped straight towards the police barrier.

The policemen and women saw the car pull out and accelerate up the wrong side of the road towards them. A couple of them put their arms up in the air, waving them back and forth for the driver to stop. The waving faltered when they caught sight of the young girl in the front seat, hunched over the wheel, a look of grim determination on her face.

One officer drew his weapon.

'YEEE-HA!' Trey shouted when they were no more than a few metres away.

Alexa wanted to tell him to shut the hell up, but she was concentrating too hard on not losing control of the fast-moving vehicle. She'd never driven at more than 40 mph before, and the car handled totally differently at this speed.

The policeman with the gun had taken up a position right in the centre of the road. He'd adopted a shooting stance and managed to fire off one round before he realized that they weren't going to stop and that staying where he was wouldn't be good for his long-term health. He leaped clear of the car moments before it crashed through the barrier, a climax of noise filling the air as metal shrieked and glass shattered.

They were through. The car lurched sickeningly to one side, and Alexa had to fight with the wheel to keep control. One of the rear tyres burst, and the loud noise of reinforced rubber repeatedly smacking into the tarmac filled the car.

'You did it!' Trey said over the noise.

Alexa was silent. Her face was as white as her knuckles as she gripped the steering wheel. She was shaking.

Trey decided it would be a good idea to keep quiet. He turned in his seat at the sound of sirens. Peering out through the rear screen he could make out the three police bikes, which had begun to pursue them up the road.

The car was incredibly difficult to control with only three good tyres, and Alexa thanked her lucky stars that there was no other traffic on the road. She slewed round a bend, the car making a terrible din that momentarily drowned out the howling sirens from the police bikes behind them. She glanced in the mirror.

The lead rider in pursuit was no more than ten metres behind the car now, flashing his lights at her. The police officer accelerated, bringing his bike up beside the car and pointing a gloved hand at her to pull the car over.

Trey grinned and waved back at him from the passenger seat.

194

'Stop antagonizing them!' Alexa shouted.

'I was just being friendly.'

They could make out the turning they had to take up ahead. Alexa steered the car over as far as she could on to the wrong side of the road, trying to give herself the best possible chance of making the corner at speed in a car that was pulling alarmingly in the other direction. Then she forced the wheel over, causing the car to shake and moan in protest. Trey glanced behind him again and saw a shower of tiny yellow sparks flying out behind the vehicle as the steel rim of the back wheel ground against the tarmac.

They made the turn. Alexa swore out a long string of expletives as she battled to keep the car from crashing. And then they were on the long, straight stretch of Fulham Road. For one second they forgot the police pursuing them, forgot that the car they were in was so dangerously damaged, their gazes drawn to the skyline visible between the buildings up ahead. Even from here Leroth and the Shield looked indomitable.

'Stop the car,' Trey said, looking down the road and seeing the way blocked first by abandoned vehicles, then by a wall of people.

'The police . . .'

'I'll get rid of them,' he said in a low voice. 'There's no other way through. Stop the car.'

Alexa braked to a halt.

'We'll have to take the final stretch on foot,' Trey continued. He frowned, thinking things through. 'It's only about six or seven hundred metres to the beginning of the Shield. Can you make us invisible?'

She shook her head. 'Not if we're moving. If we were stationary, yes, but—'

'Then you're going to have to hang on to me. I'll give you a piggyback. Just give me a minute to get rid of these guys,' he said, motioning with his head towards the three police bikes which had pulled up behind them. One of the officers stayed on his bike, barking something into his radio. The other two dismounted, and started to walk towards the car.

'Stay in the vehicle, sir,' one of the cops called out when he saw Trey climbing out of the passenger door.

Trey ignored him and turned to face them.

'Get back in the car please!' the lead officer shouted, reaching for something on his belt.

Trey knew there was little point in trying to reason with them. He and Alexa had committed goodness knows how many offences, and he suspected that telling the officers that they needed to get into that thing up the road to try and save the world from a zombie epidemic wasn't really going to wash. Instead, he Changed.

The policemen froze, watching in horror as the overall-clad boy turned into a monster before their very eyes. The werewolf took a step forward, lowered its head and roared.

The officer who was still mounted on his bike dropped his radio and put the vehicle into gear, twisting the accelerator and spinning the bike round so that smoke billowed off the rear tyre in a huge blue-grey cloud as he sped off. The other two ran. They simply turned on their heels and ran as fast as their legs would carry them.

Alexa climbed out of the car, shaking her head in Trey's direction.

The lycanthrope shrugged and then walked round to her, turning away and dropping down on one knee so that she could mount his back.

'This is crazy,' she said into his ear.

Trey concentrated on the spell that would allow him to 'talk' back.

Crazy actions for a crazy day, eh? Now hold on tight because this is going to be a rough ride.

Alexa held on for all she was worth, wrapping her arms about the huge werewolf's neck and gripping with a force that would probably have strangled a human, but seemed not to bother the massive lycanthrope at all. As soon as she was on his back he leaped forward, his long rangy strides eating up the ground. The roofs and bonnets of abandoned cars that blocked their way caved in beneath the combined weight of the werewolf and his human passenger, as Trey jumped on to, and then over, them. It was only when they approached the back of the crowd that Trey slowed a fraction. Everyone was looking ahead at the giant supernatural hemisphere when Trey let out an almighty bellow, sounding like a great male lion roaring across the savannah. The people turned en masse and faces already filled with fear took on an even more terrified look – then everyone scattered before him.

Trey kept up the noise, running straight through the middle of the crowd. People must have thought the young girl on the creature's back had taken leave of her senses and attacked the beast, leaping astride it to try and throttle it. But nobody stepped forward to assist her.

The police barrier posed about as much hindrance as the forsaken cars had, and Alexa cried out as Trey jumped again, simply soaring over the heads of the officers who'd been standing there. At the sight of the werewolf, the police and the crowd ran in panic in the opposite direction, those that had refused to leave earlier, despite the protests of the police, finally deciding that enough was enough.

Trey ran on for another hundred metres before he stopped, crouched behind a deserted police van, and allowed Alexa to climb down.

She grinned at him. 'Crude but effective.'

The werewolf winked back at her. *A bit like your driving.*

They paused and looked up in awe at the hellish, zombie-filled dome that had been dropped smack in the middle of London. Alexa was about to say something when she heard somebody call her name. She looked off in the direction of the sound. Behind a mangled wreck of a car, not far from the Shield wall, was one of the Maug guards that her father had been speaking to earlier. The demon – Alexa could always see nether-creatures for what they really were – was kneeling over a crumpled figure at the kerbside.

198

'Hag,' Alexa said in a whisper as she hurried in the sorceress's direction.

The old woman lay on her back, clearly in terrible pain and unable to get up. She managed to raise a hand, which Alexa took in her own.

'You made it,' the old woman said in a small voice. She glanced over Alexa's shoulder and managed a toothless smile in the direction of the seven-foot lycanthrope standing there. 'And you managed to get your werewolf back.'

'Thanks to you.'

The old woman waved the remark away. '*You* performed that magic, not me. I doubt I'd have been able to combine those spells.' She coughed and tiny crimson pearls flew into the air before settling back on her lips and chin.

'We need to get you away from here,' Alexa said. 'We need to—'

'You need to be quiet and listen,' the old woman said, fixing the girl with an icy stare. 'Your father is in there. I got him in. And I did as he asked and got as many people out of there as I could.'

She coughed again, wincing in pain as she did so.

'Your father cannot defeat Caliban *and* Helde alone. You and the lycanthrope boy must get inside to help him.'

Alexa nodded. 'Tell me how to breach the Shield. Tell me the magic and I'll—'

The old woman stopped her with a wave of her hand. 'You're a skilful and powerful sorceress, Alexa, and I've enjoyed teaching you in the short time we've been together.

But even a teacher as good as me could not teach you the sorcery required to breach that thing in the time we have left.'

'But—'

'I will open the Shield again. For you and Trey.'

'You're not strong enough, Hag.'

'I'm strong enough to do this one last thing.'

Alexa frowned as she took in what the old woman said. 'No.' She looked down at the broken body and tried to stave off the tears that threatened. Hag portrayed herself to everyone as a bad-tempered and disagreeable old harridan, but during their times together Alexa had seen beyond this, and come to know the sorceress as she truly was. She hated to see her like this.

'Goodbye, Alexa,' Hag said, and then turned to nod at Trey. 'Take care of her, lycanthrope. And remember that you have the power within you to put an end to all of this.' She motioned with her hand in the direction of the dome. 'If you come up against Helde, you must remember that her heart is the only surviving part of her. Destroy that, and you destroy the sorceress.'

Alexa shook her head. 'Hag . . .'

But the old woman ignored her. She'd already closed her eyes and begun intoning the words necessary to perform her final act of sorcery.

28

Caliban stood at the exit to the tower and scanned the area before him. This was going to be far too easy. He stopped for a moment and considered. If everything went to plan, this was how he would feed in the future – from a herd of entrapped stock that couldn't run and couldn't escape. There would be no hunt, no need to use the vampiric powers and qualities that made him and his kind reviled and revered in the Netherworld. He would become little more than a consumer. He hissed at himself, pushing these thoughts away, angry that he'd allowed them to creep in. The anticipation of fresh, warm blood helped to dispel any doubts he might be having about his plan, and he forced himself to concentrate on what he had come out here to do – to feed. The vampire deliberated. He wanted something young and vibrant and female. Yes, a meal like that was exactly what he needed now.

He cast his eyes about. In a car parked about fifty metres away from him he sensed what he was looking for. She was hidden from sight, but the vampire knew the young woman was there. He opened his mind some more.

She'd locked herself in. She'd been about to get out of her car and go into her flat when that vast black tower

materialized. Then she'd watched in terror as those vile,
undead creatures had appeared and attacked the people.
Her mobile was dead, and so was the car: turning the
keys in the ignition had elicited nothing at all. It was as
if the entire thing had ceased to function as soon as that
monstrosity had appeared. It was an older car, a classic
VW Beetle. She'd never been so glad in all her life to have
doors that locked mechanically via buttons you depressed
at the top of the door sill, instead of a system that relied on
the car's electrics.

She'd pushed those buttons down with fingers that shook
so badly she could hardly work them. And she'd checked
again and again that they were fully depressed before
clambering into the back of the vehicle, pulling the travel
blanket she kept on the rear seat over her, and hiding in the
footwell between the front and rear seats.

The vampire laughed quietly to himself and strode out in
the direction of the vehicle.

When he came alongside the car he bent forward,
peering in through the side window at the uneven blanketed
thing huddled on the floor. He thought about tapping on the
glass with his talons, just to see what the response might be.
The vampire was in a playful mood. He smiled as a better
idea came to him. Caliban misted, disappearing from where
he'd been standing on the street and reappearing in the front
passenger seat of the old car. It wasn't easy translocating
himself from a standing to a sitting position, but the ancient
vampire performed the feat without too much effort.

'You look rather foolish beneath that blanket,' the vampire said.

The muffled scream behind him brought a look of grim satisfaction to the nether-creature's face. He ran his tongue over the tip of a fang, testing it. The car stank of fear, and the smell excited the vampire, making him all the more eager for the coppery, warm blood he craved. He'd always liked to toy with his food a little before feeding on it.

'I'd like you to come out now, please.' He paused for a second. 'If you do not come out, I will be forced to physically remove you from your pathetic hiding place. And that could get a little . . . unpleasant.'

He smiled again when he heard her moving to get up on to the seat behind him.

The woman shook violently as she stared at the thing in the front seat of her car. She pushed backwards with her legs, pressing into the leather rear seat, trying to put even this tiny additional distance between her and the creature. How it had got into the car she had no idea. The locks were still down, and she'd have heard if the doors had been opened. It was as if the thing had appeared out of thin air. Right now she could only see the back of the creature's head. It was a human head; bald with a greyish-white skin stretched so thin that a criss-cross map of blue veins could clearly be seen. Despite its appearance, she knew that whatever was in the car with her was not human. As if sensing this, the vampire turned to face her. Ghastly yellow eyes glared out at her from deep-set orbs, and the creature's top lip pulled back to reveal the fangs that promised nothing but death. She opened her mouth and screamed, the fear-soaked sound filling the small space of the car so completely that it hurt her ears. Caliban threw back his head and laughed. He reached out a hand to grab her.

There was a thump on the window quickly followed by another. The vampire, momentarily distracted, flicked his eyes towards the source of the sound. A zombie stood outside the car. Caliban cursed under his breath. Unless he was very much mistaken, it was the mounted police officer he'd seen felled from his horse earlier. The undead creature was missing an ear and had bite marks all down one side of its face. Its nose was also missing, an ugly black and scarlet hole in the place where it had once been. But it was clear that the wound to the erstwhile policeman's abdomen had been his undoing: most of the creature's lower intestines were hanging loose from a great fissure in its body just above the leather belt it wore. It carried these slippery, gore-covered tubes as best it could in one hand, using the other to bang on the car roof while letting out a loud moan.

The woman screamed again.

'Shut up!' the vampire commanded, all hint of amusement now gone.

The combined sound of the woman's cries and the zombie's moans attracted another undead creature. The newcomer might once have been an attractive woman, but now her looks were that of a corpse. Her neck had been broken so that her head hung back at a strange angle, forcing her to peer down her chin to see ahead. The second zombie joined the first in banging repeatedly on the roof of the car.

Caliban cursed under his breath. Looking out through the front windscreen he could make out more of the creatures, drawn by the noise, beginning to make their way towards the car.

There was no way the vampire could feed now. He was very particular about when and how he fed, choosing whenever possible to do so in private, and the thought of drinking from this girl beneath the derelict gaze of these mindless monsters filled him with utter revulsion. He could simply kill her – rake his talons across her throat and shut her up for good. That would get rid of the revenants at least – he'd seen how quickly they lost interest in their victims once they were dead. But the lust for blood still gnawed away at him, and he knew that the sight of the gore in this state could produce an undesired effect in him, leading him to go on a murderous rampage. No, he needed to control his anger and desires.

'I won't kill you,' Caliban said. He nodded at the zombies outside the car. 'But they will.' He paused, then added, 'For a little while, at least.'

He opened the door beside him, forcing it against the undead body of the ex-policeman, and barged his way through the frenzied push of the zombies. He walked away to the sound of the woman's screams as the creatures tore at each other to get at her inside the car.

The vampire hissed in anger and frustration. He turned

his head to look up the road. There were more humans hiding up ahead – he could already sense some of them. Maybe he would have to make a house call to get some privacy. He paused for a moment, glancing up at the tower behind him, momentarily remembering the promise he'd made to protect Helde.

I won't be gone long, he told himself. *She'll be fine.*

29

The few zombies that Lucien and his party encountered when they'd crossed through to the other side of the Shield had been dispatched quickly. The undead ignored the demon and its vampire master, heading straight for Tom with an unerring single-mindedness. With so few of them out here by the perimeter, it was simply a matter of positioning Tom behind them so that the vampire and the Maug could put the pathetic and unfortunate creatures out of their misery with one or two swings of the blades they carried. The Maug had been a little slower to react than it should have been and received a nasty-looking bite to its arm – luckily it was only a flesh wound and the zombification process that brought humans back from the dead did not apply to nether-creatures. Nevertheless, it was clear that the revenants would attack anything in their path that tried to stop them getting to their prey.

When it was over Tom looked down at the decapitated bodies, reminding himself that not too long ago they'd been living humans. 'Poor bastards,' he said with a shake of his head.

They moved on up the road, taking care to check the side streets, alleyways and shop doors for any undead that might be lurking there or on the verge of reanimating.

'We should decapitate all the bodies,' the Maug said, gesturing with the machete in its hand at a cadaver in the road. 'That way they won't come back to life and be behind us as we move on.'

Lucien walked over to the body. It was that of an elderly man. 'This man was not a victim of a zombie attack,' he said. 'He appears to have been crushed and trampled underfoot. He'll stay dead.'

'We can't check every body we come across to assess the cause of death,' the Maug said. 'It would be safer to just lop off their heads and—'

'We will not be "just lopping off the heads" of the dead!' the vampire said, staring at the creature. 'This man had a family. Friends. When this,' he gestured about him, 'is all over they will come to try and find him. How do you think they'll feel when they find that somebody has "*just lopped off his head*"?'

The Maug mumbled something under its breath and looked down at its feet.

'We need to make our way to the tower,' the vampire said.

'I'm assuming it'll be much worse there,' Tom said.

'That's where they were released from, so yes, I'm guessing that's where the fatalities were the most numerous. If I'm right, after that initial attack everyone would have spread out to the perimeter of the Shield. Others will be in hiding. It'll be slower for the zombies to locate their victims now. But if the ones out here are reanimating, I think it's safe to say that more will be reawakened the nearer to the centre we get.' Lucien looked at his friend. 'You, like every other human inside this place, are most vulnerable,' he reminded him.

'And that is why I'm the bait in this here fishing trip. You need me to draw them out.'

'Just stick behind us. You and I,' Lucien nodded at the Maug, 'will flank him. Between us we should be able to deal with whatever comes at us. We need to get to the tower and stop Helde. If we neutralize her, the Shield will cease to function and all those infected but not turned yet will be saved that fate. There's nothing we can do for those poor souls who have already reanimated except put them out of their misery.'

'Aren't you forgetting someone?'

'I'll deal with my brother if and when he shows up. My guess is that he's safely holed up in the tower too, watching his handiwork. But there's not much keeping him here now. Now that the zombies are reanimating, he can simply up and leave. We don't have much time.'

'Then let's quit yapping and go,' Tom growled.

30

The new opening in the Shield that Hag managed to create for Alexa and Trey was small. They stood before it for a moment, and then the werewolf stooped forward, bending at the waist, and hurried through.

He crouched, tense and alert, fully expecting to be attacked by something or someone as soon as he was on the other side. He reached out with all of his lycanthrope senses, hoping to anticipate the danger he was certain awaited him. The smells and colours were those of the Netherworld that he'd experienced when he fought in the Demon Games, but the human roads and the structures that lined them looked alien bathed in the purple light. There was no sign of any other living creature on the street. He glanced down at the severed body of the Maug lying on the floor, and the creature's dead eyes stared straight back up at him. The sight of the demon sent a cold shiver through the teenager and he correctly guessed that it must have been bisected when Hag's first opening had crashed shut.

The lycanthrope turned, noticing that Alexa had not yet followed him. He quickly bent down again and peered back through the breach. She was watching Hag. The old woman was on the ground where they'd left her, her body shaking violently with the effort of performing the sorcery necessary to create and maintain the opening.

You have to come through now, Lex, or all her effort will have been for nothing.

He watched as she turned to look at him, tears running freely down her face.

Now! Before this thing shuts!

She nodded, took one last look at the sorceress and ducked through the gap.

The last Maug demon didn't join them. They'd agreed the creature would stay behind until Hag died and arrange for her body to be taken back to Lucien's building. The nether-creature had not needed too much persuading.

No sooner had she ducked through the opening than it disappeared behind her.

Alexa felt Hag's death like a physical blow. Attuned to the energies of the magical plane as she was, she felt something collapse and fall in on itself, like a vast building being demolished with dynamite – the sense that something had been lost, and at the same time released, forever. The young sorceress gave a little gasp and turned to look at Trey to see if he too had felt it. It was clear he had not, but the look on Alexa's face must have told him everything he needed to know.

Has she gone?

'Yes.'

She took a deep breath and told herself that now was not the time to mourn the loss of Hag. She glanced at the Shield again before turning her attention back to Trey. 'That's it,' she said. 'We're trapped in here now. There's no way out unless Caliban and Helde move elsewhere or they're stopped.'

Trey nodded. He was looking up the road at two bodies lying there.

'What is it?' Alexa asked.

By way of an answer, Trey walked over to the corpses and peered at them intently.

'Trey?'

It looks like Tom and your father didn't have the unchallenged entry that we did. These bodies have had their heads removed. Zombies.

'Then they can't be too far ahead of us. We should go.'

The lycanthrope nodded. The tiniest movement caught his eye, and he turned to look up at a window above a tailor's shop. The old man peering from between the gap in the curtains quickly stepped back into the darkness of the room behind him.

These people have seen things that will haunt them forever, Trey thought. He turned and looked at the girl by his side. *Let's try and find your father and help put an end to this madness.* He sniffed the air, and the synaesthesia he experienced in his lycanthrope form transformed the smells and scents around him into vivid pictures inside his head – a pictorial landscape of olfactory information. Lucien's scent was like a silvery-black fog, whilst Tom's was more solid in appearance and had a distinct golden colour. His mind's eye

212

painted these colours and shapes on to the landscape around him so that he could clearly make out the path the two of them had taken up the street.

Their scents are still very fresh.

She nodded, and the two of them set off after the others.

31

The carnage around the dark tower was, as Lucien had said it would be, much worse than anything that he and those with him had come across on the way there. During the short journey from the Shield's perimeter they'd had to fight off several frenzied attacks from already reawakened dead and even as they did so, more of the creatures were reanimating all around them. They passed two or three streets and walkways that spurred off the main road and led up to the football ground itself, and these were full of zombies all heading in the direction of the colossal sporting arena that loomed over the houses and shops around it. Luckily, the people inside the stadium had managed to close the doors and barriers that provided entry to the ground, but the revenants seemed to sense that the place was teeming with human life, and were drawn to it like iron filings to a magnet. Lucien glanced up one of these walkways and could see thirty or forty zombies converging on a glass-fronted entrance hammering unrelentingly at the smoked glass panels. Lucien knew that the draw of the stadium to the undead creatures was working in his group's favour, and that their progress would be much harder and slower if all these zombies were roving the street they were making their way along.

But there were still zombies roaming around and in many ways these were the most dangerous. They would skulk in shop doorways or behind parked cars that lined the roads, and it was Tom's job, situated between the vampire and the Maug demon, to draw them out. He sang an old Irish folk tune in a loud voice as they walked, the sound of the human voice luring the stragglers towards them so that they might be put to rest by the swinging blades.

'I don't think they like your singing, Tom!' Lucien commented at one point when a trio of zombies had come running up the road towards them. The zombies moved quickly, but in an erratic and jerky manner, as if the signals from their brains were being sent in short, broken bursts. When the undead creatures were almost upon them Lucien and the Maug sprang into action, the vampire catching one of the attackers by the throat and holding it at arm's length while he dispatched another. Then he shoved the first zombie off, releasing his grip on its neck, and swung the blade again to intercept the creature as it renewed its snarling, gibbering attack. The revenant's head joined those of the other two on the road at the group's feet.

Tom was about to make a smart remark about Lucien's own vocal skills – it was often joked about back in the apartment that the vampire had the worst singing voice any of them had ever heard – when the hairs on the back of his neck stood up. He turned in time to see the body of a man they'd just passed reanimate, the zombie jumping to its feet and rushing at him, both arms outstretched before it. The Irishman pivoted on his foot, bringing his machete up in a vicious upward arc that sent one of the creature's forearms spiralling off into the air before hitting the ground with a dull thump. The creature didn't falter for a second; it was as if the force of the blow and the subsequent loss of a limb was of no consequence to the revenant. With its one good arm still outstretched, it raked the Irishman's face with hooked fingers until Tom brought the machete down from its elevated position, burying the blade deep in the zombie's head, cleaving it almost in two. Gore spattered up into Tom's face, and he wiped it away with his sleeve as the creature sank to its knees, dead for the second time that day.

Lucien heard the commotion, and turned to look at his friend just as the zombie fell to the floor. 'Are you all right, Tom?'

'Everything's dandy. Just had to fight a little rearguard action is all. It's about time I had something to do – I'm running out of songs to sing.'

The two friends grinned shakily at each other, but as they did so Tom spotted something over Lucien's shoulder that caused a bolt of pure terror to tear through every cell in his body. The vampire, noting the sudden change in the Irishman's facial expression, turned to look in the same direction. But beyond the carnage that was all about them he could see nothing that might have caused such a reaction.

'Tom?' Lucien said.

'He's here. He's out here on the street.'

Lucien turned to look again. 'Who?'

'Your brother. Caliban. I just saw him go into a shop door up there.' Tom nodded in the direction he was still staring.

Another zombie – Tom guessed it had been a woman, but it was difficult to tell with the state of the thing – clambered out of the back of a VW Beetle car and came charging at the group, shrieking loudly and attacking them from the front with mindless abandon. The vampire almost distractedly swung his heavy blade to behead it.

'Did he see us?' Lucien asked, referring to his brother.

'I don't think so,' the Irishman said with a shake of his head. 'He had his back to us. He seemed in a hurry . . . agitated.'

Lucien nodded. 'He's hunting. Witnessing all this bloodshed has ignited his hunger. He never was able to control his lusts.' As he said this there was the sound of a human voice calling out to them, and the group spun about. The look of fury on the vampire's face as he spotted his daughter running towards him was terrifying to behold. Trey, in his lycanthrope form, was loping alongside her, his eyes scanning in all directions on the lookout for any sign of danger.

She stopped in front of them, breathing deeply through her mouth.

'What are you doing here?' Lucien snapped.

'We've come to help.'

'Did I, or did I not, specifically tell you not to come here?'

'Yes, but I never agreed I wouldn't.' She gestured with her head at the huge lycanthrope by her side. 'Anyway, we're here now.'

The vampire looked from his daughter to his ward. 'Hello, Trey. I would say it was good to see you, but that hardly seems appropriate given the circumstances.'

'He'd been captured . . . kidnapped.' There was an accusatory tone to Alexa's voice that was clear for them all to hear.

The vampire considered this for a moment, then looked back up at the werewolf. 'It is good to see you. I'm sorry I ever doubted you.'

Trey shook his massive head, and when he broadcast his thoughts it was to the vampire alone. *There's no need to apologize, Lucien. Thank you for sending Alexa out to try and find me. It was my fault that we came. I persuaded her to bring me. I have to be here, you know that.* He looked about him at the chaos. *This is the beginning of the end that the legend spoke of. The legend about me.*

The vampire's gaze fell to Trey's broad chest.

'Where is the amulet?' he asked.

Around the neck of a friend of mine. She's dead, buried beneath the rusting wreck of a car. He stared intently at the vampire. *I don't need it any more.*

Lucien smiled gravely at the teenage wolf. He opened his mouth as if to say something else, but stopped, turning instead to glare once more at his daughter, who smiled

218

sweetly back at him. 'If and when we get out of this, you are grounded for a month!'

'But—'

'Look,' said Tom in a loud voice. 'Right now we're in the middle of a zombie swarm, the devastation of which has drawn our sworn enemy out of that tower and into one of those buildings up ahead. Would it be too much to ask you two to shelve this little altercation and concentrate on how we put an end to this nightmare?'

Lucien sighed. He glared at his daughter one last time before turning his head to look in the direction Tom had just indicated. 'We'll have to split up. One group must go into the tower to try to find and neutralize Helde, while the other group goes after Caliban. I was hoping that they would stay together in there,' he said, nodding at the black citadel, 'but it looks as if they've separated.' He frowned, and turned to Alexa. 'I'm assuming the effort to maintain all of this,' he looked up at the dark purple sky overhead, 'requires an immense amount of concentration.'

Alexa knew what her father was thinking.

'She'll have to enter a deep, trance-like state. She'll be vulnerable. I'm guessing she was counting on Caliban to look out for her.'

He nodded to himself, working everything out in his head. He looked at his daughter again as something occurred to him. 'Have you encountered any undead on your way here?'

'Just one, but Trey quickly dealt with it.'

'Did it attack you?'

'It seemed unsure. It didn't come at me like the ones we saw you dealing with just now.'

Her father nodded. 'It's as I thought – you're only half human, so the zombies' reaction to you is not the same as it is for Tom. Nevertheless, I don't want you out here in the open. I want you, Trey and Tom to go into the tower to find Helde. Kill her. Bring this Shield down and stop this infection spreading further. I will go after my brother then come to help you.'

I'll go with you.

'No you will not, Trey.' He held a hand up to stop the teenager. 'You and Alexa make a powerful team. You'll need to look out for each other in Leroth.'

'You're not going after him alone!' Alexa said, staring in horror at her father.

'I have the Maug here to help me.' The demon shifted from foot to foot as if embarrassed by the vampire's reference to it.

Wait a minute, Trey transferred his thoughts directly into the heads of Lucien, Tom and Alexa at the same time but his eyes were fixed on the Irishman. *The infection is spread from a bite or zombie blood entering the human bloodstream, like through a wound. Is that right . . . ?* The others turned their heads, following Trey's horrified gaze.

'What?' Tom asked in a strange voice, his hand reaching up, fingers tracing the cuts on his cheek that the zombie had

220

made just before he'd dispatched it. He didn't need to ask them if the gore which had spattered him as he lopped the creature's head off had got into the wounds – he could see it by the look on their faces. 'Ah shit . . .' he said.

We need to get moving. We need to eliminate Helde before the infection takes hold of Tom.

Lucien placed a hand on his friend's shoulder. 'Don't worry,' he said. 'You're not going to turn into one of them.'

'Oh, I *know* I won't. I'll use *this* on myself before I let that happen.' He lifted the machete in the air with one hand.

Lucien stepped forward and hugged his daughter, looking up at Trey, who was standing behind her. 'Take good care of her,' he said to the lycanthrope, who nodded back at him. He watched them turn and walk off in the direction of the tower. Once they'd gone some distance he addressed the huge Maug demon standing by his side.

'I want you to go back to the football ground where we saw that huge gathering of undead and dispatch as many of them as you possibly can.'

'But you just told Alexa—'

'We can't have that many zombies roaming about the place if we're successful in pulling this Shield down. You'll be able to eradicate most if not all of them without too much trouble.'

'But—'

'I will be fine. Now go.'

The vampire watched as the demon shuffled away. Turning, he directed his attention to the shop his brother had entered. He had the element of surprise, for now at least. He nodded to himself, and walked off up the road towards the stop.

32

Trey, Alexa and Tom paused for a moment, peering into the darkness that was the opening into the solid rock that formed the outer defences of Leroth. Trey had been inside these passages before, but on that occasion the entrance had been created by Gwendolin, in a different location to this one. There was no natural opening to the tower; entry and exit could only be gained if a portal was opened from the inside.

Although nothing was said, Trey was aware that the other two were looking to him for guidance. *There's a series of tunnels inside. The last time I was here Charles had a map, but we'll just have to see how we get on.* He paused before reluctantly adding, *I'll lead the way.*

The werewolf stepped into the darkness and immediately reeled as the stench hit him.

Trey didn't need his acute olfactory sense to tell him that this was where the zombies had been waiting: the bloated, rotting stink of them filled the air, so strong it made him gag. When he'd recovered he looked behind him and beckoned for the others to join him. Reluctantly he latched on to that fetid smell – to Trey it appeared as a greenish-brown miasma that disappeared off up the passage to his right.

'What in the name of all that's unholy is that smell?' Tom said as he stepped in behind Alexa.

Death. We need to go to our right.

'Can you see anything in here, Trey?' Alexa asked. 'I could give us some light if you want.'

I can see well enough to get us safely through. I don't think it's a good idea to light ourselves up in any way. If anything is lurking ahead in these tunnels it would know we were coming. Just place your hand on my back. Tom can do the same to you and we'll go in single file.

In this way they slowly made their way forward, Trey following the trail and retracing the path that the zombies had taken through the maze of corridors. Something else had been with them – something that had escorted them here to wait for their release. Trey had no idea who or what this escort may have been, but its scent reminded him of the waft that is thrown up when a large rock or log is suddenly turned over – the smell of damp, mouldering earth and burrowing insects. There was something else to it, something ancient and primeval, and this caused an involuntary shudder to knife its way down the lycanthrope's spine. They walked on, Trey following the trail until he detected the merest hint of a breeze coming from somewhere up ahead. His first instinct was to hurry towards it and escape the stench which still made his stomach roll and lurch, but he slowed to a halt instead, causing Alexa and then Tom to stumble into the back of him.

'What is it?' Alexa hissed.

I think there might be an opening ahead, Trey said, broadcasting to both Alexa and Tom.

'Good, then let's go.'

Wait.

Trey allowed himself to remember the last time he'd been in this place, and the terrible things that had happened here. Then, he'd been with the young sorcerer, Charles, and they'd been attacked upon leaving the tunnels and entering the inner bailey on the other side.

There's a bailey beyond these tunnels that we have to cross to get access to the tower itself. It used to be guarded by small winged demons, but Charles killed them all when we were last here. There are two doors, which can only be opened with sorcery set into the base of the tower, one on either side. I didn't come in this way before, but I'm guessing it's directly opposite the exit of these tunnels.

Trey knew that the trouble with using the spell was that his emotions were laid bare to those he was communicating with, and that Alexa and Tom would be all too aware of the paralysing sense of fear he was experiencing right now at the thought of returning to that black tower. Mixed in with the fear were the feelings of guilt and remorse at how his friend had been killed by Caliban and his sorceress Gwendolin, and how Trey had been powerless to help him.

Alexa placed her hand on his back, and he could feel the warmth of it through his fur. 'It'll be OK,' she said.

'We should get moving,' Tom said in a low voice.

Trey and Alexa could clearly hear the discomfort in their friend's voice.

The Irishman leaned his forehead against the cold tunnel wall, resisting the urge to lift his fingers to his cheek. The side of his face that had been gouged by the zombie was already burning with a heat that made it pulsate with pain, and he could feel the infection spreading down his neck. His joints were beginning to ache, as if he was in the early stages of influenza, and he was shocked by how quickly these symptoms had manifested themselves. There was one thing of which he was certain: things were going to get much, much worse. He tightened his grip on the handle of the machete and tried not to think about what the outcome would be if they could not get to Helde in time. Part of him wanted to scream at Trey and Alexa to get moving, to stop procrastinating and get into that tower. But the military man inside him knew that they were doing the right thing: proceeding with caution to ensure that they did not simply hand over the element of surprise to their enemies. He took a deep breath and let it out slowly through his mouth.

Are you all right, Tom?

'I'm fine,' the Irishman said. 'Don't you worry about me, lad.'

He's not fine, Alexa said to Trey, and he guessed that she was 'broadcasting' only to him. *I can feel the heat coming off him. The infection is taking hold.*

Trey looked round at his friend. Even in the darkness, he could see how terrible Tom looked.

Let's go. He turned, ready to lead the way again, when he caught the merest suggestion of movement up in the deep shadows overhead. He was about to bring this to the attention of the others when they were attacked.

The passageway was filled with the sound of the werewolf's roar as he felt the muscular tentacle tighten round his neck. With one jerk he was lifted up, his feet leaving the floor as the suffocating grip on his neck was increased. Trey managed to get one hand between his throat and the constricting appendage, pulling as hard as he could to allow himself to breathe. With his other hand he attacked the thing, raking his claws into the blubbery flesh until another tentacle wrapped itself about this wrist and yanked his arm up and back. He could see more of the tentacles falling from a vast black mass overhead, reaching for Tom and Alexa.

Look out! There's something on the tunnel roof above us! It's already got me! RUN!

Trey watched as a black tentacle formed into a noose above Tom, ready to be dropped over the Irishman's head.

Tom! Overhead now!

Trey, his eyes beginning to bulge from the pressure applied round his neck and throat, could only stare ahead helplessly as the Irishman swivelled and swung the machete round in a tight, fast arc about his head. The blade easily sliced through the tentacle, which dropped to the floor with a loud flopping sound. There was a terrible scream from overhead, and Trey got his first look into the mouth of the creature attacking them. The large circular opening, set into the underside of the thing clinging to the roof above them, dilated outward in all directions, giving the werewolf a glimpse of the ring of deadly looking teeth lining its circumference. Behind these a thick black tongue flapped about. And around this foul orifice were the creature's eyes: eight huge black discs sunk into the flesh stared unblinkingly down at its prey.

'Light, Alexa! We need light! Now!' Tom shouted out, staring about him blindly in the dark.

The grip on Trey's neck was tightened further and his own knuckles, jammed between the snake-like noose and his windpipe, crushed his airway. He was lifted even further from the ground and his vision began to dim as a grey curtain pressed in from all sides.

Help!

Suddenly the light that Tom had demanded filled the tunnel. Alexa stood, looking like a goddess holding a small sun, her eyes screwed up in pain from the sphere of dazzling bright light hovering over the palm of her outstretched hand. The effect was immediate and startling – the black thing clinging to the roof of the tunnel let out a long, piercing ululation. All of the tentacles, including the two that held Trey, were withdrawn in an effort to cover the large black eye-globes set around the mouth. The creature moved incredibly quickly, flowing back along the tunnel and disappearing into the darkness.

Once released, Trey had fallen to the hard floor where he'd crumpled into a heap. Now he stood gingerly, rubbing at his throat, gasping in deep breaths of air. Alexa was looking at him as though she were ready to finish the job that whatever the thing on the roof was had started.

'Remind me *not* to listen to you in the future, Trey Laporte,' Alexa said with a shake of her head. 'What was it you said? "I don't think it's a good idea to light ourselves up in any way. If anything is lurking ahead in these tunnels it would know we were coming."'

How was I supposed to know that that thing was in here? It wasn't last time!

'Well, neither were Tom and I, but we're here now! And a good job we were because that thing was about to throttle the life out of you!'

I was fine. Another few seconds and I'd have got free.

'Another few seconds and your head would have been stuffed into that big mouth!'

'The main thing is that we're all all right,' Tom said, wiping the surface of his blade against his trouser leg.

Trey didn't say it, but Tom looked *anything* but all right. The Irishman must have read his mind. 'When I say all right, I mean that thing didn't kill any of us. And look on the bright side – even if it had, only two of us would have *stayed* dead. I'd have been up and about in a matter of no time.'

Alexa shook her head, unable to keep from smiling at the older man's grisly humour. 'I vote we keep the light on until we get out of these tunnels. Any objections?' She looked from one to the other. 'Good. Now let's go and find Helde and put a stop to all of this.'

33

Lucien slowed as he approached the shop that his brother had entered. It was a furniture store: an expensive designer chair with a huge elaborate lamp hanging over it dominated the window space. The interior was dark but his eyes travelled up to the windows above the shop. He tuned into the space, probing it with a predator's instincts. There were humans up there – humans who had watched the horrors unfold in the street outside and were now clutching each other in terror, too scared to move in the prison that had become their home. He could *feel* their despair.

Lucien hissed, cursing his brother for what he had done here. This was the world that Caliban wanted – a world of fear and subjugation, a world in which he and others like him could hunt freely and murder innocents. He was about to try the door when he felt a now familiar dropping sensation, as if a hole had suddenly opened up in the floor beneath him.

He was inside the shop.

He paused at the door at the rear of the storeroom, sensing the people in the flat above, their fear almost palpable to him. It was delicious, that fear, and it brought a smile to his ancient face. He reached out and tried the handle, knowing

231

it would be locked. He would mist – disappear on this side and reappear on the other. It was dangerous to do so. Vampires rarely used their teleportation powers unless they could see the place where they intended to rematerialize – there was no telling what might be waiting on the other side of a wall or door and to reappear in the middle of a solid structure would be disastrous. But the need to feed was so strong now that he knew he would take the risk, and he was about to do so when he stopped. Something was wrong. He had the uneasy feeling that he was being watched. He turned round and crept back through the storeroom to look out of the front of the shop –

Lucien stepped back, flattening himself against a car, just in time to conceal himself from Caliban's gaze.

The ancient vampire stood, unmoving, just inside the entrance to the shop. He was in complete shadow and knew that he could not be seen by anyone looking in. He stayed like that for a few moments, stock still, all senses reaching out. Nothing moved in the street. He would have to go out and investigate. Better to be safe than sorry.

Lucien knew he had seconds before Caliban appeared. He turned and spotted a zombie shuffling up the road towards him. There was no sign of the furious, lurching charge that he'd witnessed earlier. It seemed simply to be walking aimlessly about, no doubt hoping to stumble upon any humans that might be in the vicinity.

Lucien did the first thing that came to mind: he grabbed

the walking dead creature, spinning it about so that he held it out before him, his hands on its shoulders. The zombie groaned and struggled weakly against the vampire's attentions, trying to shrug him off with a series of jerky, disjointed movements. Lucien shoved it towards the window.

Caliban was on the verge of misting to the outside of the shop when the zombie appeared at the window. It stumbled forward, hands and face pressed against the glass for a moment, smearing the surface with drool before turning and shuffling off again.

'Damn these creatures,' Caliban hissed.

He cursed himself at the same time. He was on edge and he'd allowed these shambling, brainless revenants to get to him. They were a nuisance. First they'd stolen the delicious morsel that he had trapped in the car, and now they were bothering him again while he was on the hunt. This one must have been what he'd sensed spying on him – though it had felt more sinister than that. But it must have seen him enter this place and followed him. He spat, shaking his head in disgust.

'The sooner I can feed and we can get out of here, the better,' he said to himself, turning and walking back towards the door that led to the flat overhead and the hot-blooded creatures he would feast upon.

Lucien cocked his head to one side, listening. He considered misting into the interior of the shop and pursuing his brother, but he quickly ruled this out – first he had to get to the people upstairs to warn them of the danger heading their way. He eyed the first-floor window. Like his brother, he was well aware of the risks of reappearing in something solid. He visualized the space behind the window, hoping that it was empty, held his breath and disappeared.

34

Alexa and the others emerged from the tunnels, stepping out into the inner bailey. The tower loomed over them now like a giant obsidian dagger that had been thrust hilt-first into the ground, and they looked up in horror at the gibbets hanging from numerous points around the structure, many of which were occupied by the corpses of nether-creatures in various states of decay. Trey kept his eyes glued to the skies, half expecting an attack from the small winged demons that had descended on him the last time he was here with Charles. None came, but Trey was still anxious to get inside the tower and away from this place – this had also been where Caliban had attacked them as they'd made their escape and where Charles had given up his life to save Trey.

Come on, the lycanthrope said, taking Alexa by the elbow and steering her towards the base of the tower. It was clear to them both that Alexa would not need to use her sorcery skills to unlock the huge door set into the tower wall – it was open, no doubt left that way by the vampire when he'd gone out to prey on the human population outside.

Trey and Alexa stood on the threshold, nervously looking into the dark interior. They were about to step inside when a low, almost inaudible groan behind them made them turn, and what they saw made them hurry back in Tom's direction. The Irishman looked awful: he was sweating profusely, and the side of his face where the zombie had gouged him was distended and had taken on an ugly purple colour. One eye was almost swollen shut, the white surrounding the iris and pupil flooded with blood. The overall effect was horrific and shocking.

Tom waved away their offers of help, but neither of them was fooled by his insistence that it probably looked a lot worse than it felt. Staying close by his side they moved into the interior of the tower.

The layout to this entrance was very different from the one on the other side of the tower through which Trey and Charles had entered. That one opened up into a large chamber, the walls of which were packed with cells. It was where Trey had first encountered the battle-angel Moriel. The entrance on this side was simply a huge square column that disappeared up into the tower above. Stone steps lined the sides, each set made up of about twenty stairs before a small landing turned to its right and the next set of steps began. They could only make out the first four or five stages, the rest disappearing into the darkness overhead.

'Look,' Alexa said, walking over to a hatch set into the floor. It was open and she peered down at yet more stairs that led down under the tower. She frowned for a moment, and then turned to look at Trey and Tom.

'There's powerful magic at work somewhere down there.

I can feel it.' She nodded into the darkness. 'That must be where Helde discovered the source of the Shield.'

'Which way do we go? Up or down?' Tom asked.

Trey hooked into the smells at the base of the tower, working through the visual trails they overlaid across his vision. That ancient and unpleasant stink of rot and decay that had accompanied the zombies was here too, and it was clear that whatever creature had left that scent had used the hatchway Alexa had found. But the most recent trail painted by that particular odour led up the stairs.

I think she's upstairs, he said. *My guess is that she's somewhere near the top of the tower. That's where Caliban's rooms are.*

Alexa nodded at Tom. 'You should wait here while we go up.'

'Now just a moment, young lady. If you think I'm too—'

'I don't think you're too anything, Tom. I think that we need a rearguard at the base of the tower to protect us against Caliban in case he gives my father the slip and re-enters Leroth behind us. If that happened we wouldn't have a clue he was here until it was too late.'

Tom looked at her. He knew that she was taking pity on him and trying to save him from the exhausting climb ahead. And in truth he doubted if he would be able to make the ascent in the state he was in. All of his joints ached constantly, the pain in his back and legs was becoming unbearable and his head ached so badly that he was finding it hard to concentrate on anything but the simplest of tasks. He also knew that Alexa was posing the offer in such a way that he wouldn't lose face.

'Since when did you become this great military strategist?'

'I had a great teacher,' she said.

The Irishman managed a smile. He flipped the machete in his hand, catching it deftly by the blade so that the handle was pointing in the teenage girl's direction. 'Here, you should take this,' he said.

She shook her head. 'You'll need it. As I say, what if—'

'Yeah, yeah, I know. Caliban and all that.' He nodded at the proffered handle again. 'Take it. If you don't I'll have to insist on coming up there with you.'

With a little shrug Alexa reached forward and took the fearsome-looking weapon from her friend.

'Besides, when have you ever known me not to tool up properly when out on a mission?' The Irishman gave them both a wink with his one good eye and fished around behind his back in the folds of the long coat he was wearing. He swung out a small crossbow, which had been hanging from a strap around his shoulder. It was pre-loaded with a nasty-looking barbed bolt, and mounted on top of it was a device Trey recognized as a laser sight.

The werewolf grinned at his friend, his long pink tongue lolling from his mouth as he did so. *I thought you said those things weren't easy to fire accurately?*

'That's true, but you know what they say – practice

makes perfect.' He winked at the werewolf again. 'I'll stay here and watch your backs.' He turned to look at Alexa. 'It does make sense, so we'll pretend that that's the only reason I'm staying put down here.' The affection he felt for them both was now clear to see in his expression. 'Watch out for each other, and don't do anything I wouldn't do.' Alexa went to say something but he waved her off. 'Go on now. Go and get that mad witch and put a stop to this lunacy. Otherwise the next time you see me I'll probably be trying to eat your brains or something.' And with that he sank down against the wall facing the entrance, the crossbow propped on his knees, ready to fire.

35

Alexa was taking another brief break in her climb.

The stairs seemed to go on forever. Flight after flight wound up into the darkness. Occasionally, on one of the small square landings, she and Trey would find a door, but they'd opted to ignore these, Trey insisting that they follow the trail of the scent he was convinced was Helde's. The ascent was much harder for Alexa. Trey's huge strides easily carried him up three steps at a time, and he made the climb with very little exertion. In contrast, the young sorceress's thighs burned with the effort of it, and she needed to rest at regular intervals.

Like the tunnels, this place was almost completely dark. Alexa supplied her own light; this time the orb she held in the palm of her outstretched hand was about the size of a golf ball and threw only a small amount of light ahead of her so that she could make out the steps. Even so, it would shine out like a beacon to anyone or anything looking down from above, so whenever she was forced to stop as she had now, Trey would disappear into the darkness of the higher levels, scouting ahead to ensure that there were no nasty surprises waiting for them.

Alone in the darkness, Alexa's thoughts turned to her

father and the danger he must be in right now. She tried not to imagine what would happen when he caught up with his brother. And then there was Tom, sitting down there alone at the entrance to this place, infected by a member of the undead and doomed to join them should she and Trey fail in their mission to stop Helde. She got to her knees and crawled to the edge of the landing, peering down into the blackness. The light she held did nothing to illuminate the ground level, but she could make out the dim purple glow of light that spilt in through the doorway.

'Tom?' she hissed down as loud as she dared. 'Tom, are you OK?'

There was no answer.

Are you mad? Trey asked as he loomed into view, coming down the stairs towards her. The sound in her head was harsh and loud, and she could tell from the dark patterns that accompanied the words that he was cross with her.

Look, I'm as worried about him as you are, but giving us away right now is stupid. We're nearly there! There's a final door after just six more flights.

Alexa groaned, and the lycanthrope stretched out a clawed hand, placing it gently on her shoulder. *Are you going to be OK? Look, I don't know why you don't just take me up on my offer and let me piggyback you up. It's not a problem, Lex.*

'You can't help acting the he-man, can you? No thank you, I'm quite capable of walking the rest of the way. Having come this far, six more flights isn't going to kill me. I just have to keep telling myself that I'm back at the gym on the Stairmaster and not in a translocated part of the Netherworld heading towards certain death.' She smiled at him and he grinned back.

Stop being so stubborn. You should be conserving your strength. Who knows what we're going to face up there. Let me carry you.

She looked up into the darkness and puffed out her cheeks. 'Oh, what the hell. OK, you can carry me. Happy now?'

He nodded, and as he did so his features became serious. *I just wanted to say, before we go on. You and me . . . I—*

'Don't,' she said, reaching out to touch his arm. 'I know how you feel, Trey. I feel the same way about you. Let's just get this over with, and then . . . well, let's see what happens, OK?'

The lycanthrope nodded.

'And I think you should stop using the thought transference spell until we find Helde. I'm sure she's far too busy holding the Shield in place to monitor for other forms of magic being used near her, but there's no sense in chancing it, is there? I can do without this if you're carrying me the rest of the way.' She extinguished the little ball of light she held, and then reached out in the darkness until she found his hand, slipping her own into it. He knelt down and she climbed up on to his back for the second time that day.

In this way the two of them made their way through the inky void to the topmost levels of Leroth.

The staircase ended in a short corridor that led to a metal-studded wooden door. Alexa climbed down and the two of them approached it, pausing for a moment before reaching out and pulling it open. There was light on the other side, provided by burning torches held in sconces on the walls. Trey's heart beat a little faster as he realized he'd been in this passageway before. He and Charles had entered it from another direction, but this had been where they'd found the doors that led to Caliban's rooms and next to these they'd found Gwendolin. Other memories, unbidden and painful, came flooding back to him and he closed his eyes for a moment, doing his best to extirpate them.

As if sensing his distress and discomfort, Alexa squeezed his hand with her own. 'It's going to be OK,' she said in a barely audible voice that betrayed her own fears and concerns.

The lycanthrope nodded. He pointed a finger away to his right and led her up the corridor in that direction.

Trey stopped in front of the door where the trail finished. He could still make out that smell of decay and corruption as it leached its way through and around the door.

'This it?' Alexa whispered.

He nodded and reached for the black metal hoop that served as a handle, pushing the door open to reveal the source of the stench on the other side.

36

Caliban misted, reappearing on the other side of the door that separated the storeroom from the living quarters overhead. He paused for a second, allowing his mind and body to come back together – the moments immediately following a translocation were always very uncomfortable, and it took him a few seconds to quell the feelings of sickness and disorientation that inevitably resulted. Misting was also extremely draining – he had done too much of it already on this hunt – and Caliban felt himself weaken even further now. He was in a small hallway. Before him was a wooden staircase that led up to the apartment. The vampire wondered if he could simply walk up them without one of the treads creaking or groaning. He wasn't particularly concerned about making a noise, in fact the terror that such a thing would strike into the hearts of the young couple above would be delicious, but it wouldn't do to draw this out too much. No, he would get into the apartment, feed, and then return to Leroth.

He was keen to leave London now; he had succeeded in the first phase of his plan to bring the human realm to its knees, and had done so in a way that sent a message to his pitiable brother, showing him that he could strike anywhere at will, even in the city that Lucien considered to be his stronghold. He had to admit it – the Shield was a great asset. Helde had been right to insist on finding it. He briefly considered the sorceress and how he had left her, alone and vulnerable, back at the tower. He would get back to her as soon as he'd fulfilled his own needs.

He went to the top of the stairs and reached out to open the panelled door that led through to the living space on the other side.

Jenny Lassiter clutched her fiancé, Matt. They sat together on the sofa, unmoving, where they'd been for the last hour or so. She thought that they must both be in shock. Neither of them had spoken in some time. They just sat, holding each other, staring intently at the window, beyond which the world had been transformed into a living hell.

She glanced at the telephone. Nothing worked. Every appliance had simply ceased to function when that black tower had arrived and the sky had turned into the terrible dark purple firmament which hung over them now.

Even though she knew it would be pointless, she was about to suggest that they try to call the police again when she felt Matt stiffen and turn to stare at the door behind them.

'What is it?' she asked in a tiny voice.

'I thought I heard a noise. Out there.'

Jenny's heart hammered in her chest. She could feel the panic spreading through her at the thought that one of those undead creatures they'd witnessed running from the black tower into the crowd might be inside the house with them. She clutched at Matt, pulling him to her with hands that shook violently.

She wanted to scream, but her body wouldn't respond to any of the commands her brain sent to it. She froze.

And then two things happened at once.

The door to the living room flew open, revealing a ghastly, nightmarish creature. It peeled its lips back, displaying a pair of terrifying fangs, and glared at them with yellow eyes that shone with a ferocity terrifying to behold. The look it gave them left them in no doubt that they would die at its hands. And then its eyes darted towards the window, its expression changing from lustful malevolence to one of shock, and then fury.

Jenny turned to see that another of the creatures appeared to have simply materialized out of thin air, this one in front of the window. There was a fraction of a second when the two supernatural beings regarded each other. The one at the window allowed the tiniest of smiles to play at the corners of his mouth, and then said something in a voice so low that it was difficult for Jenny's human ears to pick it out. She thought it might have been, 'Hello, brother.'

The vampire at the door screamed out in fury and attacked.

37

Lucien reappeared in the first-floor apartment over the shop, just in front of the window he'd eyed from the street. Despite his momentary disorientation following the mist, he relished the look of shock on his brother's face when he appeared at almost the very instant Caliban stepped through the doorway. His brother's reaction, and the momentary inaction it caused, was enough to buy Lucien the time he needed to recover, but he'd lost the element of surprise, and now his vile sibling was hurtling across the room towards him. Lucien didn't hesitate. He hefted the heavy-bladed weapon he still held and swung it hard, aiming for his attacker's neck in a blow he hoped would decapitate the onrushing vampire.

There was a blur of movement as Caliban brought up his hand in a futile attempt to block the blow. Lucien had already witnessed how the honed blade was capable of carving through muscle and bone, and he knew that it would not be impeded on its deadly path. But he'd forgotten about the metal prosthesis that his brother now wore since his hand had been severed at the wrist by Trey when they'd first met. The blade hit the artificial limb, and a harsh, sharp sound, accompanied by a vampire's wail, filled the small room. The vibration the blocked blow sent back along the metal blade and through its handle was enough to force Lucien to let go of the weapon, which clanged to the wooden floor, where it stayed. The metal hand had succeeded in preventing the blade from reaching its intended path, but in doing so it had been wrecked: the rods that ran along the back of the hand and into the wrist had all broken so that the bladed fingers hung uselessly, and the hand itself was twisted back at an odd angle. Undeterred, Caliban threw himself at his brother, driving his body forward with his legs so that he was now in a headlong dive, arms outstretched, teeth bared and aimed at his enemy's exposed throat.

Lucien reared back, and at the last second managed to shove his hand into the side of his brother's face, deflecting those deadly fangs from their intended target. The shift in his own weight, combined with Caliban's irresistible forward momentum, lifted Lucien off his feet, and he found himself flying backwards towards the window he had just appeared in front of. He grabbed hold of Caliban, determined that if he was to plunge to the street below his brother would be joining him. There was a cacophony of smashing glass and splintering wood, and the two vampires crashed through the window. They continued to kick and strike each other as they fell, both knowing that the hard, uncompromising concrete was rushing towards them.

There was the sickening snap and crunch of bone as they landed. The impact forced them from each other's grip, and both vampires covered up as best they could against the deluge of heavy glass daggers that rained down on them from above. The deadly torrent added to the terrible injuries they had already suffered from the fall and their exit through the sheet glass window. Blood the colour of tar flowed freely from their numerous deep, ugly wounds.

Lucien knew he had to get up. With a great effort he rolled over on to his knees and forced himself to stand. He looked up and was not surprised to see that his brother had also managed to get to his feet and was turning to face him. Both vampires were in a terrible state. Lucien allowed himself the briefest of mental checks to ascertain the degree of his own injuries. He knew he had several broken ribs, and that his left shoulder was dislocated. The bones in his right foot were smashed to pieces. His left cheekbone and skull were almost certainly fractured, and blood ran freely from a wound in his head, making him blink repeatedly to keep his vision clear. He could feel his body starting to mend, but knew from the extent of his injuries that this would be a slow process. Despite the pain and discomfort he was in he allowed himself a half smile when he saw that his brother was, if anything, in an even worse state. The wrecked hand hung uselessly from one arm and his left leg was twisted at an impossible angle so that his foot pointed inward towards the other. One of Caliban's ears had been completely torn off, and the gore that poured from the wound had already soaked through his clothes. A huge shard of glass stuck out from his abdomen, and Lucien watched as his brother wrapped the fingers of his good hand around the offending

249

object and yanked it free, throwing it to the ground where it shattered into a hundred pieces.

'You look terrible,' Caliban said, spitting a globule of blood to the pavement, his eyes never leaving those of his brother.

'You look worse.'

Caliban nodded as if knowing this to be true. He appeared to be utterly exhausted, wavering on the spot like a drunkard. Yet his eyes burned with a terrible intensity as he took in his sibling. 'So this is the end, brother?'

Lucien nodded. 'This is the end.'

'Are you ready to die – again? It will not be like before, Lucien, when I gave you my blood to bring you back to life as a vampire. If I had known then that I would create the traitor before me I would have left you to rot.'

A strange smile crept on to Lucien's face, accompanied by a look of defiance that he knew the other vampire found unsettling. 'I've already died twice at your hands. What makes you so sure I can't come back a third time?'

Caliban narrowed his eyes at his brother, small frown lines creasing his forehead. 'What are you talking about? Died *twice*?'

'Exactly what I say, brother. The last time we fought you bit me – here.' Lucien pointed to the shoulder that Caliban had sunk his teeth into during their last battle in a derelict factory in the Netherlands. 'You poisoned me. I don't know how – perhaps you are so corrupt and foul now you are nothing *but* poison. The wound became more and more infected until eventually I . . . died. But Trey stole Mynor's Globe from you, and Alexa used it to resurrect me.' Lucien angled his head to one side, raising one eyebrow slightly as if mocking the other vampire. 'You didn't know that, did you? You thought we took it simply to stop you using it. That really is rather sloppy of you. Almost as sloppy as leaving your sorceress unguarded and all alone up in that portable monstrosity over there.' He gestured towards the tower with his head, but his eyes never left those of the creature standing before him. 'So I ask you again, what makes you so sure that you can kill me, brother?'

'You're lying. What you say is impossible.'

'Everything about *us* is impossible. You've created a new monster, brother.' He drew his lips back to reveal his fangs. 'Haven't you stopped to ask yourself why these have grown back? And what about my new trick of being able to see inside your head, hmm? That must be a significant inconvenience to you. There are other changes – more profound even than those – that have befallen me too.'

Caliban went to say something and stopped. His eyes took in the tower for a second before switching to the dome-like Shield overhead. Despite the dark purple gloom that existed on this side of the Shield, he could clearly make out the sun in the sky on the other side. He took one last look at his brother and disappeared.

Lucien wheeled round on the spot looking for his brother, expecting one last attack. He was surprised when he saw that Caliban had appeared some distance away from him and was now trying to run back towards the tower, despite his ruined leg making this almost impossible. In spite of everything, Lucien found a tiny sliver of admiration for his evil brother; he knew that he did not have the energy to mist again, and yet Caliban had somehow found the strength to do so. He set off after his sibling, his own ruined foot making progress agonizingly slow, determined to stop him from reaching the safety of Leroth . . . and Alexa and Trey.

38

Tom sat alone in the gloom at the bottom of the tower. The sound of Trey and Alexa's footsteps ascending the stairs had long since faded to nothing, and now an oppressive silence pressed in on the Irishman like a physical force.

He was in the grip of a terrible fever – shaking with cold one moment, his skin on fire the next. His clothes were wet with sweat, and an appalling smell came from him which made him wish he were out in the open. The pain in his face, neck and shoulders was unbearable; molten metal had replaced his blood in these places and he groaned with pain as it continued to spread further into tissue and organs. He wouldn't last much longer. He allowed his eyes to close and his head to fall back against the hard stone wall he was propped up against.

He was on his feet and racing up the stairs, taking them two at a time. He could sense them ahead – the boy and the girl. But they were unaware of him pursuing them until it was too late – until he'd leaped at them from behind and dragged them to the floor where he ripped and clawed at the flesh of their throats and—

He awoke with a start, the sound of his own terrified shout echoing back at him through the shadows. It was happening. He was losing his humanity, and becoming one of those nightmarish creatures he'd seen and fought outside. It was inevitable. He would soon slip into unconsciousness, and when that happened what limited options he currently had would be gone.

He'd been close to death before. On numerous occasions he'd wondered how his life might end, but *this* had never been one of the ways he'd imagined – alone and scared at the bottom of a dark stairwell, his life slowly ebbing away, each moment bringing nearer the terrifying prospect of becoming one of those things. He wouldn't allow that to happen.

He looked down at the crossbow in his lap. It was cocked and loaded with a short but lethal aluminium bolt. He would use it. Use it before it was too late.

39

Helde sat, slumped in the black obsidian throne, struggling to maintain the sorcery she had created all about her. She could feel her strength slipping away along with her grip on the forces necessary to maintain the Shield. In her mind she continued to occupy the place of dark magic, where she still imagined herself as a huge spider at the centre of the web that was the Shield, but she knew it was time to return to the human realm and the vile physical body she now inhabited. She must return, dismantle the Shield and move on. She allowed a part of herself to drift away from the place of sorcery and return to her physical body. And the second she did, she knew that she was no longer alone. She was in danger, and her guardian had failed to keep her safe.

Trey and Alexa stood in the doorway looking at the nightmare creature sprawled across the throne. These were Caliban's rooms, and the place was cold and stark. The sickly, coppery smell of dried blood filled the place, so that Trey initially recoiled at the stench that painted black shadows across his vision. Open windows set into the walls looked down on the scenes of death and destruction below, and even at this height the screams and moans of the dead and dying reached them.

It was their first sight of the sorceress, and even though they knew Caliban had returned her from the grave, the manner of her resurrection took them both by surprise. 'Helde,' Alexa said in a whisper, nodding towards the thing, which seemed to be entirely composed of tiny insects. 'So that's how Caliban brought her back.' She wrinkled her nose up. 'I think I'd have preferred to remain deceased.'

The sorceress was apparently unaware that they were in the tower, let alone the room. The sound – almost like white noise – of hundreds of thousands of hard, chitin-covered bodies crawling over and into each other came from the sorceress's body, and were it not for this constant movement of the invertebrate host, Trey and Alexa might have believed the prone creature before them was dead.

They glanced at each other.

Is this a trick? Trey asked, reasoning that there was no longer any need not to use the thought transfer spell.

Alexa shook her head. 'It's taking so much effort and concentration to keep that Shield in place, she's had to abandon her physical self and enter another realm. She wasn't expecting to be left alone like this. She couldn't have known that her guardian would abandon her at the first whiff of fresh blood.'

They stepped further inside the room until they stood at the small dais on which the stone chair sat. They looked at each other, and Trey nodded towards the machete hanging from the strap round Alexa's wrist. *We should get this over with,* he said.

He watched as Alexa wrapped her fingers round the handle of the weapon, slowly bringing it up before her so that the tip pointed at the nether-creature. Her eyes went from the blade to its intended target, and she took a deep breath as if to steady herself, but made no further move towards the thing. She stood there, the end of the deadly blade wavering in the air, incapable of making the final thrust.

Trey knew what was stopping her. Helde was, right now, utterly helpless. He knew that in the same position, with the knife in his hands, hc would be having the same difficulties. But then his thoughts turned to Tom, alone and dying in the darkness at the foot of the tower – dying from an infection that this creature had let loose on this realm. He thought of how his friend and mentor would become a thing of horror, and how the Irishman had threatened to take his own life rather than let that happen. This thing in front of him was responsible for that. It was responsible for the screams reaching them from below, and if it was not stopped, would be responsible for ending the world as he knew it.

Do you want me to do it? he asked, stepping forward and gently putting his hand on Alexa's shoulder.

'No, I'll be OK.'

The heart. Remember, it has to be the heart.

Alexa nodded and took a step towards the prone figure. She drew the blade back, aiming for a spot in the centre of the chest. She thrust her hand forward . . . just at the very moment Helde became aware of the danger she was in. That death was rushing towards her.

The blade never found its target.

Helde's mind snapped back into her physical body a split second before she was about to be killed for the second time in her very long existence.

Several things happened at once.

Helde's grip on the Shield, and her ability to hold it in place at its current size, was lost. She was about to abandon it altogether when it occurred to her that she had no idea how big this attack force was. She did the only thing she was able to, and reduced the Shield's size to the area immediately surrounding the black tower. Instead of a great sprawling dome, the Shield became a tight, cylindrical cone which was easier to keep in place. At the same moment that she did this, she used a simple spell to deflect the steel blade which was heading towards her chest, so that it struck nothing but a solid wall and careered away from its murderous path. Helde had done all of this without once moving from her hunched position on the throne. Now she lifted her head for the first time and took in the two intruders. The huge werewolf must be the boy Caliban had spoken of, and the girl must be the dhampir daughter of the vampire, Lucien Charron. The ancient sorceress only had seconds to take this in – she was under attack, and she must fight to stay alive.

Helde thrust her hands, palm out, towards her assailants,

sending two great balls of energy towards them. She was weakened, but she knew that even these simple weapons should be enough to put an end to those who had dared to attack her in this way. Her magic was swatted away as if it were no more than a fly however, and the two sorceresses locked horns as their energies met – in the same way that Helde and Hag's had met when they fought over the breaching of the Shield.

The lycanthrope took it upon himself to attack, the great brutish creature lunging forward with its teeth bared. The sorceress threw up her hand again, and the werewolf flew backwards through the air, smashing into a wall with so much force that the stonework around him cracked and broke. Helde turned her attention to the dhampir again, and was taken by surprise; she had not expected the newcomer to be so versed in the magic arts or to be so strong and skilful. It occurred to the ancient creature that she might not have the strength to defeat this newcomer – she was too depleted, too run down. Again she considered abandoning the Shield, and again she rejected the idea. Whatever happened, she had to protect Leroth – it was her only means of escape.

Helde took the only route open to her – if she couldn't defeat her attackers in her current form, she would have to take on another. She knew she had neither the time nor the energy to summon up a creature from the Netherworld, so she turned to the nearest thing she could: the creatures that made up her body, the thousands of insects that encased her ancient heart and allowed her to live again.

She would use them to defeat the humans intent on killing her.

Trey managed to get back to his feet just as Helde stood for the first time. He watched as she threw her arms up into the air and issued a terrible high-pitched scream, before dropping to her knees. She collapsed forward, her forehead connecting with the cold stone floor with a dull *thunk*. Her forearms rested slightly out ahead of her on the flagstones, her back hunched and curved over her legs. She looked for a second as if she were praying to a divine spirit or perhaps about to beg them for mercy.

Somewhere far below them, outside the tower, the unmistakable sound of two vampires' primal screams, accompanied by a crashing and splintering of glass, made its way up to them. Even from this height, they could hear the pain and fury in those terrible howls. Trey glanced across at Alexa and it was clear from the way that her body had stiffened that she too had heard the noise. Their attention had only drifted for a moment, but when they looked back at the sorceress she'd already transformed into a horrifying hell-beast.

The host of insects that made up the sorceress's body had grown suddenly, swelling in size ten- or twenty-fold before fusing and merging together so that instead of a host of individuals, one huge armoured carapace was created. The vast black shell sat in the centre of the room, unmoving for a moment, until three pairs of vicious-looking barbs appeared along its sides. These grew quickly outwards, transforming as they did so into articulated insect legs which scrabbled at the floor and lifted the exoskeleton up from it. As swiftly as the legs had appeared, the vast head emerged from the front of the shell. Huge black orbs glared down at the intruders, and below these were three rows of pincer-like mandibles which snapped together, filling the room with a terrible *clacking* sound. Beneath the mandibles was the mouth, and this was opened to display the rows of 'living teeth' housed there: hanging from the jaws, attached by their barbed tails, were large scorpion-like creatures which writhed about.

If the thing they'd first encountered when they'd stepped into these rooms was a grotesquerie, then this new entity was nothing short of an abomination. The thing let out a terrible screech and charged.

Alexa reacted first. The wall of energy that she summoned up in front of herself and Trey was just strong enough to withstand the attack as the nightmare creature slammed its hard, chitin-covered shell into it. The teenager gasped at the force of the blow, flinching uncomfortably and screwing up her face as if she had herself been physically struck. Despite her pain, Alexa managed to keep the barricade in place as the giant beast crashed into it for a second time. But this time Alexa went on the attack; as the creature reeled she allowed the wall to drop and lifted both hands, linking them at the thumbs and shouting out in an ancient tongue as a stream of liquid fire poured forth from her palms. It was one of Hag's spells – she had taught it to the young sorceress but they had never had time to try it out together. Alexa gasped with astonishment at the force and power of the spell, and Trey watched her struggle to stay on her feet as she moved her hands back and forth, painting the now unmoving creature in a liquescent inferno so hot that he could feel the hair that covered his body begin to singe and burn. The flames stopped as suddenly as they'd started, and the young sorceress looked across at her handiwork.

That terrible head and face, along with the limbs, had been retracted into the shiny carapace as soon as the first flames had left Alexa's hands. The chitin-covered outer shell was still burning as small flames licked across its surface, giving off a foul-smelling smoke that filled the room.

'Well, that went better than I expected,' Alexa said. She grinned at Trey but it was clear to the lycanthrope that the sorcery had taken a lot out of her. He went to say something when he caught a hint of movement from the corner of his eye. He turned to look at the smouldering shell, and sure enough something was moving about inside.

I don't think she's dead, Lex. I think she's—

There was a terrible shriek, and that malevolent face appeared at the opening of the shell again. Trey shuddered at the triumphant look in the creature's eyes. The legs emerged next, but this time it didn't charge as it had before. It drew back its head and spat at the young sorceress.

Alexa managed to get her arms up in front of her face as the shower of black scorpions struck her. She screamed out as they grabbed hold of her flesh in their pincers, their whip-like tails arching up and over to stab her with toxins before she could pull them off and throw them to the floor. The pain and damage they inflicted was not terrible: they were merely a distraction. The giant insect thing lowered itself and prepared to charge, the vicious mandibles at the front of its face snapping together with renewed ferocity as it did so.

In her bid to overpower the other sorceress, Helde had momentarily forgotten the lycanthrope.

Trey charged forward, his terrible roar filling the room. He leaped up at the hideous face, wrapping his arms about the section behind it which disappeared into the shell and twisting his body so that he mounted it from the top. He squeezed with all of his might and sank his huge jaws down into one of those eyes, biting as hard as he could into the tough exterior. There was a scream from the creature that was Helde, and she tried to retreat into the safety of that armoured shell again, but Trey was ready for this; bracing his legs on either side of the casing, he thrust his weight forward in the other direction, and continued to strangle and bite.

Helde reached up with her front legs, flailing wildly at the werewolf and opening up terrible wounds on Trey's flanks with the sharp spikes that crowned them. But the lycanthrope would not be shifted – he felt a new power and assurance in his actions. This was part of his destiny after all. If anything the pain of the wounds spurred him on, and he tightened his grip even more, howling with the effort of choking the life out of the hell-beast until its struggles became weaker and weaker and it finally crashed to the floor. Only then did Trey relinquish his grip and slide back to the ground. The lycanthrope dropped down on to all fours, his tongue hanging from his blood-caked mouth, as he sucked the unpleasant air into his lungs in great, rapid breaths.

'Trey? Trey, are you OK?'

He looked up to see Alexa on her feet again. Her arms were covered in bleeding wounds, and it was clear that she'd been stung in several places – large angry-looking swellings covered her hands and arms.

Yeah, he said, straightening up. *I'm fine. A few cuts and bruises, is all. How about you?*

'Not great. I feel like a human pincushion, but I think the worst of it has worn off now.' She half grimaced, half smiled at him.

There was a moan from the floor, and they both turned to look at Helde. The hell-beast was gone, and she'd returned to her former physical state, or at least, some of her had. Apart from those that comprised the head and torso, the multitude of insects that made up the sorceress no longer seemed capable of adhesion. Struggle as they might, the host could not mould themselves together in the humanoid form as they had previously, and the thing on the floor moaned out loud as it writhed around, a limbless trunk to which the groaning head was attached.

264

'You've got to hand it to her,' Alexa said, nodding down at the wretched thing, 'she doesn't die easily.'

A low and terrifying growl came from somewhere deep inside Trey's chest. *We'll see about that,* he said. The lycanthrope walked over to the dying sorceress and reached down to grab her by the neck, ignoring her agonized cries as great chunks of her fell away. He walked to the window. Thousands of the tiny creatures scurried after him and streamed up his legs and body. They flowed along his arms and hands, and rejoined the black mass hanging from his grip as if still intent on knitting her back together again.

Trey looked down from the window and saw the two vampires.

He'd got there just in time.

40

Despite the agony that each step caused, Lucien had almost caught up with his brother, whose response was to hurl vile abuse and threats back over his shoulder in his sibling's direction.

'You are a traitor to your own kind, Lucien! A vile and despised quisling who is hated by those who once trusted him. I will have you tortured for a thousand years. You will beg me for death, but I will not give you that satisfaction! Oh no. I will—'

They were no more than ten metres from the entrance to the outer tunnels when Lucien threw himself forward, grabbing his brother from behind and dragging him to the floor.

The two vampires set about each other again, rolling across the paving stones, clawing and biting and tearing undead flesh from each other's bodies with tooth and claw. The fight was vicious and unrelenting, each of them intent on killing the other to put an end to their rivalry forever. Despite his wounds, Caliban slowly gained the upper hand. He was stronger than Lucien, with a hatred inside that fuelled him to fight, even with his wrecked and broken body. Little by little he became aware of his brother's weakening state. He feinted with his broken metal arm, looking for an opening, and when he saw it he lashed out with his other hand, fingers hooked so that his talons flayed open a horrific wound across Lucien's face that caused him to cry out and stagger back. Caliban threw himself after the other vampire, using his wrecked metal hand as a bludgeon and smashing it repeatedly into Lucien's head until his brother's knees buckled beneath him. Forcing Lucien on to his back, Caliban leaped upon him and continued to rain down blow after blow until there was no longer any resistance. With his good hand he forced Lucien's head away, viciously twisting his skull and pressing it down into the blood-drenched paving stones so that his neck was exposed.

'Goodbye . . . brother,' he said, eyeing the flesh he would rip out with his teeth. 'It seems you weren't quite as difficult to kill as you thought.' He reared his head back, ready to deliver the final deadly bite. As he did so, the dim glow of the sun on the other side of the purple overhead vault made him blink and wince for a second.

From high above came the unmistakable roar of a werewolf. The sound alone was enough to make Caliban pause, and he peered upward, trying to make out the source of the noise. Up in the highest window of the tower he spotted the lycanthrope boy, Trey Laporte. Inside Leroth? No! But he was – leaning out, his huge seven-foot frame filling the opening. One arm was thrust before him, and he held what appeared to be the head and torso of some creature he had destroyed. The vampire's keen eyes noticed the steady drip of what he first thought to be droplets of blood, only to realize they were in fact tiny black beetles.

The lycanthrope had Helde.

Caliban's mind raced through his options. If he killed his brother, the boy was sure to do the same to the sorceress. Caliban was too weak to take on the lycanthrope, and had no means of opening a portal to the Netherworld without Helde. He looked about him, noticing for the first time how the Shield had shrunk dramatically. The vampire glanced nervously towards that terrifying sun again. Why hadn't the boy already killed her? And then it came to him: it was Lucien. If the boy killed Helde the Shield would disappear and both he and the lycanthrope's precious guardian would be incinerated. For the first time since seeing the werewolf Caliban allowed the shadow of a smile to creep on to his face. He had his bargaining chip. He had his means of escape.

The vampire kept his hand firmly pressed down on the side of his brother's head. He looked up at the lycanthrope, fixing him with his pale yellow eyes.

'We seem to be in a stalemate, Laporte!' he shouted. 'I have your mentor at my mercy, you have my sorceress at yours.'

Trey roared back in the vampire's direction before taking a step away from the window. He had no intention of using the thought transfer spell to communicate with his nemesis; the idea of allowing his thoughts and feelings to be experienced by the vampire was simply deplorable. He turned to Alexa.

Caliban has Lucien, he said. *I want you to get me down there. Can you do that?*

Alexa rushed towards the window. Trey held out an arm, trying to block her so that she would not have to see the state her father was in, but she pushed it to one side and looked down at the terrible bloody tableau below. When she stepped back, the expression on her face was not one of dread, but one of grim determination. 'I think I might be able to open a portal.' She shook her head as if trying to organize her thoughts. 'They're usually created between the human and demon realms, but this place is already straddling those two places, so it should be possible.' She looked up at him. 'It usually takes hours of preparation to create these things. It'll take everything I've got to open it very quickly, and I won't be able to hold it for more than a second or two. That means I won't be able to come with you.'

Trey considered this. *It's OK. I can do what has to be done alone.*

There was a shout from below. Caliban was calling out to talk to Trey about a deal.

He nodded at her. *Do it.*

Trey leaped through the portal and emerged on the other side. He was utterly disorientated and his stomach lurched violently as the world spun around him. He still held the dismembered sorceress by the neck, and she too wailed and

269

groaned as they emerged. He staggered a little, casting his eyes about as everything slowly began to stop revolving. He saw the two vampires. Lucien was still lying motionless in a pool of blood, straddled by his brother. Caliban spotted the teenager.

'Well, well,' the vampire said, raising an eyebrow in the direction of the lycanthrope youth. 'This is an unexpected pleasure. You've come to parley.' He watched Trey's eyes as they settled on Lucien again.

'He's still . . . *undead*,' Caliban said, smiling at his own joke. He nodded at the figure in Trey's hand. 'As is Helde, I see. I'm not sure which of them looks worse. What do you think?'

Trey transformed into his human self. He stood there, naked before his nemesis, the weight of the sorceress's torso suddenly registering for the first time so that his arm dropped a little. The vampire's eyes widened in surprise at the boy's audacity.

'Let him go,' Trey said.

'If I wasn't so utterly spent, I could mist right now and be tearing the flesh from your neck before you even knew what was happening.'

'Let him go,' the teenager repeated.

The vampire tut-tutted and rolled his eyes theatrically. 'Now why would I do such a foolish thing, hmm? Even if I did have any fraternal feelings for this . . . *traitor*.' He looked down at the unconscious figure beneath him. 'I hardly think handing him over to you would be in the interests of my health, do you? You would turn back into that oversized dog-thing and finish me within moments.' He shook his head. 'I am, as you can clearly see, a little the worse for wear myself and in no fit state to put up a fight with the likes of you. No, this stalemate must be negotiated in a way that is to the benefit of all concerned. You get your precious guardian here, and I get my sorceress, or what's left of her, back. We go our separate ways and . . . *live* to fight another day.' He leered at the youngster and ran his tongue across his fangs. 'Oh, don't get me wrong, boy, I *will* kill you. I will kill you all. But not today. Not now.'

'You don't get it, do you? This isn't a stalemate at all, Caliban. You've lost. Not just this battle, but the war.'

'You haven't thought this through, boy, you—'

'Do NOT call me boy, vampire!' Trey raised himself to his full height and glared back at his arch-enemy. 'I am a son of Theiss. A true-blood lycanthrope. Remember that!'

Caliban chuckled and shook his head. 'A son of Theiss? Like your father, you mean?' The cruel smile dropped from the vampire's face and he glared up at the teenager. 'Because we all know what happened to him, don't we? I had him beheaded! *That's* what I think of your lycanthrope ancestry! Now . . . BOY, I am—'

'You're the one who hasn't thought this through, vampire. You think you hold the ace card, don't you? You think I can't put a stop to this.'

Caliban noticed the strange look on the teenager's face. There was something about that look that unsettled him.

The Laporte boy showed no signs of fear and seemed in no doubt about how this would all turn out. He watched as the youngster swivelled round and looked over his shoulder at the sun, which had started to set. When he turned back, there was a hideous smile on his face.

'I could have ended all of this upstairs. But I wanted to face you. To see the look in your eyes when you realized that the legend was to be fulfilled. I wanted to see the murderer of my parents die.' The boy continued to stare unflinchingly at the vampire. 'I'll give you one more chance to let him go.'

'You can go to hell.'

'No. But you will. Right now.'

Trey Changed. The great werewolf roared and thrust his hand through the swarm of insects that still made up the sorceress's depleted body, closing his fingers around the ancient heart at the centre. He pulled the still beating thing free, held it before the vampire for a moment, and crushed it.

Caliban watched the werewolf's huge hand close around the organ, and cried out when he saw the fine grey dust pouring from between the fingers. He looked up at the Shield which blinked once, like a light bulb about to blow, before it disappeared permanently.

The vampire screamed as the sun's rays hit him. His skin blistered; huge great boiling sores covered his face and hands, blackening and bursting almost as soon as they formed. Within seconds his skin was the colour of ash and a foul-smelling smoke seethed off him. He looked down at his brother, and his agonized screams were mixed with howls of rage when he saw that his sibling was not suffering the same terrible death. He staggered to his feet and tried to run towards the werewolf, making one last effort to kill the lycanthrope child. The vampire had taken no more than two steps when his body became a thing of fire. His eyeballs exploded in their sockets, and he screamed anew, a long belch of flame coming from his mouth as he did so. He dropped to his knees, one clawed hand still reaching out towards the lycanthrope as if, even now, he was intent on doing him some harm. The vampire pitched forward, crashing face first into the road. Flames still leaped from what was left of him – now little more than blackened bones – until these too were reduced to crumbling debris and finally dust.

Trey watched as the murderer of his parents was stirred by the breeze that blew up the London road now that the Shield was gone, and carried away to oblivion.

He walked over to the figure of Lucien Charron, bent down and picked him up, before turning and walking back into the dark tower with the vampire in his arms.

EPILOGUE

Vampires recover quickly. Within a couple of days Lucien was back to his old self, organizing everyone about him and leading the clean-up operation. And some clean-up operation it was. A military cordon was set up round that area of London – families and business were moved out of houses and premises. The few zombies that had managed to escape the Maug demon before the Shield went down were rounded up. The Prime Minister, with whom Lucien had been in contact as soon as he could hold a phone to his head again, was pulling strings on a monumental scale, working round the clock with a host of agencies to try and keep a lid on what had really happened outside the football ground on that fateful weekend. When she wasn't talking to senior officials, members of her cabinet or other world leaders, she was talking to the vampire Lucien Charron.

The number of dead was terrible. Families were contacted and informed that their loved ones had been killed in a terrorist attack. It was no lie – terror was at the very heart of what had happened that day, and now it was up to the powers that be to make sure that the terror of the Netherworld did not spread to every living person on the planet. The PM went on television, and told millions of viewers around the world who had seen news coverage of the event and footage of that impenetrable dome how the government had utilized a new type of weapon, known as an Energy Shield, to keep the effects of the attack, '. . . which was thought to be chemical in nature,' from spreading outside its cordon.

She went on to explain how . . . 'A small amount of the chemical attack agent escaped before we were able to contain it completely, and we believe this is responsible for the hallucinations of terrifying creatures that a number of people seemed to have experienced.

'Their use of high explosives in this has made it extremely difficult for us to ascertain exactly who is responsible for this outrage, but be assured that we will find out, and that the appropriate action will be taken.' She looked straight into the camera and delivered her speech, word for word, as she'd agreed to. The world watched on in appalled horror. At one point she could be seen glancing to one side of the camera, as if looking for affirmation of something or another. Out of camera shot, and unseen by the viewers, stood her advisor and scriptwriter, Lucien Charron. Next to him were his daughter and his ward, Trey Laporte.

Before the newsflash had been made the vampire and the Prime Minister had held an emergency video conference with world leaders from principal countries around the globe, explaining the truth of the situation. Most, if not all of them, already knew Lucien and they listened to what he said with interest. They reasoned that the global panic that would arise if the world's population discovered the truth – that they were, and had been for millennia, under attack from a Netherworld full of demons and creatures intent on their destruction and enslavement – was simply too much of a risk. So they'd cooked up this new story.

It was the conspiracy story to end them all, and everyone involved knew that it would take a united effort for it to work. International disputes and even conflicts were momentarily put to one side as governments, some of which had not spoken to each other in decades, promised their unified help. The alternative was too terrible to consider – a world consumed with fear and panic, mass suicides, riots and mayhem.

The task consumed Lucien. He lived in private jets, flying from country to country, talking to world leaders and officials to make sure that the truth was concealed at all costs.

Tom survived that terrible day too. He'd sat at the bottom of the tower, holding the crossbow in one hand and summoning up the courage to end it all and avoid becoming an undead freak. He'd finally made up his mind that if he didn't do it, it would be too late. He turned the weapon on himself and was about to pull the trigger when unbeknownst to him Trey ripped the sorceress's heart from her insect body and crushed it in his hand.

The effect was immediate. The agonizing pain that had invaded his tissue and bone and blood was gone in an instant. Gone. No slow, long-drawn-out recovery. Just like that, it was gone. He gasped in relief, got to his feet and looked about him in amazement as if the source of his salvation might be to hand. Then he realized the truth – that Alexa and Trey had succeeded in their mission to stop the sorceress.

He ran over to the staircase and began to climb it, hurrying as fast as his legs would carry him to the top of the tower to try and discover what the cost of his friends' triumph might have been.

Alexa was lying on the floor unconscious when Tom entered the vampire's rooms at the top of the tower. Her last act of sorcery that transported Trey out on to the streets below had proved too much for her, and she'd collapsed with the effort it had taken.

The Irishman rushed over to her and held two fingers to her neck, feeling for a pulse. It was weak, but steady. He looked about for Trey, frowning when he couldn't see him. He called out for the teenager, guessing that he must be in one of the other rooms that led off this one. The sound of his voice stirred the young girl he held in his arms.

Alexa looked up at him, the hint of a smile touching the edges of her mouth. 'You look a lot better than the last time I saw you,' she said in a small voice.

'And you look one hell of a lot worse. Where's Trey?'

'He took Helde. Down there.' She gestured with her eyes towards the window and started to get to her feet in panic.

'I don't think you should be getting up right now. You should—'

At that moment the huge figure of the lycanthrope filled the doorway, her father's bloody body draped across Trey's outstretched arms. She was rooted to the spot, unable to talk or move. She watched as the werewolf gently placed the unmoving body on a chair. Then Trey transformed into his human form, and stared back at her.

'He's alive,' he said.

She rushed to the teenager and threw her arms about his neck, kissing him as the tears ran down her cheeks.

There was a small cough behind her, and she turned to see her father, his eyes open, beckoning her towards him. She leaned down to hear him, grasping his hand.

'We need to move the tower. We need to get Leroth out of here, and quickly. Your mother's rooms are next to these. You must go there and find the information on how to translocate the tower. Go.'

An hour later, the black tower disappeared from the Fulham Road, leaving absolutely no trace. Moments later it reappeared for no more than ten seconds in St James's Park, opposite Downing Street, stopping just long enough for a wounded vampire, leaning heavily on his Irish friend, to step out on to the grass where they were met by members of the intelligence services who escorted them across the road and through the security gates which led to the Prime Minister's place of work.

When the tower disappeared again it went to a place not

in the human realm – a place where it would stay until its new owner could work out what to do with it.

Trey walked into the offices on the first floor of the building in Docklands, looking about him at the usual hustle and bustle of the place. Lucien had left Alexa, under Tom's tutelage, to run things while the vampire dealt with a number of matters in the Netherworld. He'd been gone for three weeks now. Trey didn't know exactly how long that was in Netherworld time, but he guessed it must be close to a year. Clearly the dismantling of Caliban's empire in the demon realm was taking a great deal of effort. Lucien was far from alone in his mission – the demon lords had all joined him, and agreed to reinstate the peace between the realms that had existed for hundreds of years before the evil vampire had risen to dominance. The demon aristocracy was keen to reacquire the power it had held for so long – power that had been wrenched away from them by Caliban in his quest to rule, and Lucien was working hard to help them realize this aim, all too aware that it was their best chance to reinstate the status quo between the realms. The upshot of this was that a number of nasty nether-creatures who had sided with the vampire had been popping up in the human realm, desperate to escape before it was too late. Alexa, Trey, Tom and the rest of the team in the human realm had been working hard to try and keep a lid on things, hunting these creatures down and returning them for trial.

Tom came out of the door that led to the armoury on the

far side of the office. He was carrying a Mossberg 590A1 shotgun in one hand while holstering a 9mm Glock in the harness around his shoulders. He nodded in Trey's direction and rolled his eyes. 'No rest for the wicked!' he called out. He offered the teenager a salute, and carried on walking towards the elevator.

Trey cast his eyes about, stopping and smiling when he saw Alexa remonstrating with a middle-aged man who, despite his outward appearance, Trey knew to be a terrifying-looking demon with claws and teeth that grew in proportion to how threatened it felt. He almost wished he could Change to see just how long his teeth had become as a result of the tongue-lashing he was getting from the boss's daughter right now. He walked over to them.

'. . . so if it's not *too* much to ask, I'd like you to do it again. And this time—'

'Hi, Lex,' Trey said, interrupting. 'Hi, Howard. I wonder if you could give us a few minutes?'

'With pleasure!' the demon said, casting him a grateful look and hurrying back to his desk.

'What is it?' Alexa said, turning towards him, her face displaying her annoyance.

Trey put his arms around her waist and pulled her to him. 'It's lunchtime.'

'I don't have time for lunch, Trey. There's been another portal breach and—'

'I wasn't asking you, Lex. I was telling you. It's lunchtime. I've phoned Claudia at the cafe on the corner and asked her to reserve us some of her special lasagne. I've told her to have coffees ready and that we'd be there in five minutes.' He looked at the people about him. 'This lot are more than capable of dealing with a portal breach. If it gets out of hand they can contact us on the mobile, and we can come back.'

She looked into his eyes and he watched her expression soften a little.

'You're not going to take no for an answer, are you?'

'Lucien made me promise to look out for you while he was away. That's what I'm doing. Besides, there are always going to be nether-creatures coming through to this realm from their own. We'll stop as many as we can, and deal with those that we can't. That's what we do.'

She nodded at him then suddenly leaned forward and kissed him on the lips.

'Special lasagne, you say?'

'And coffee.'

'OK, let's go.'

Alexa couldn't resist calling out some last-minute instructions to members of the team as they made their way to the elevator. They stepped inside and Trey pressed the button for the ground floor.

'I might need you to go to Oxford,' she said as the doors closed. 'There's a Shadow Demon on the loose up there.'

Trey smiled and nodded. 'I'll look into it after lunch.'

THE END

ACKNOWLEDGEMENTS

I found writing the last book in the Changeling series a difficult thing to do. And I wouldn't have been able to do it without the help, encouragement and support of some fabulous people along the way.

I'd especially like to express thanks to:

Ruth Alltimes, my new editor extraordinaire, who assuaged all my fears and proved to be every bit as wonderful as people said she would. Thank you for all your hard work and insightful suggestions. I really look forward to working with you on our next project.

My agent, Catherine Pellegrino at Rogers, Coleridge and White, for her support and good advice.

The industrious team at Macmillan who do all the behind-the-scenes stuff that makes my books possible. In particular I'd like to mention my publicist and friend Dom Kingston. Thank you for everything you've done on my behalf. I will miss you.

I'd like to thank my fans for their emails and tweets and blogs – you are a source of inspiration and joy that keeps me going when the 'worry worm' visits.

Finally I'd like to thank Zoe, Hope and Kyran for all their love. Without it I would not be able to do what I do.